Suga Baby

By: Daroncia Lowe

ISBN: 9798768742201

DEDICATION

To my family and friends who have lost someone. Your strength is admirable.

~Live in Light~

CONTENTS

Acknowledgments

Chapter One

Chapter Two

Chapter Three

Chapter Four

Chapter Five

Chapter Six

Chapter Seven

Chapter Eight

Chapter Nine

Chapter Ten

Chapter Eleven

Chapter Twelve

Chapter Thirteen

Chapter Fourteen

Chapter Fifteen

Chapter Sixteen

Chapter Seventeen

Chapter Eighteen

Chapter Nineteen

Chapter Twenty

Epilogue

About the Author

Catalog

ACKNOWLEDGMENTS

To the readers who have been with me since my first release; thank you. I appreciate your HONEST reviews and your feedback. If you're reading this, then you have chosen to stick with me, and is giving me a chance to grow with each new piece I release. Lastly, I am grateful that people still like short stories, because ya girl is one busy woman. As much as I love writing, I love serving the community, my patients and family just as much. It's a little difficult to balance the two.

It may be short, but it'll be worth it.

~Daron~

Chapter One

"Here you go, ma'am. Be careful; the plate is really hot. Would you like me to refresh your drink?"

"No, but if you could bring more rolls out, that would be great," Dahlia responded. She stuck her fork into her porterhouse and sliced the steak into bite-sized pieces. Her mouth watered the moment she opened it. Dahlia was ready to savor the juices but was interrupted by a loud tapping noise. It was the guy at the next table. "Hey, some of us are trying to enjoy our food. Stop tapping on the table before I shove that fuckin fork down your throat!" She yelled.

He continued to tap with his knife until his taps got louder and louder ***Tap... TAP.....TAP****! Her eyes opened and slowly adjusted to the daylight. She stared at the groundskeeper and plotted her next move. The steak in the dream that he'd awakened her from was the only real piece of food she would have had in a while. She was pissed that his tapping on her car window kept her from it. Dahlia rolled down her window, then stuck her head out of the car. "What is it, Mr. Jones?" She asked, wiping her eyes.

"Ms. Greene, you know you can't park here. What are you doing here this early, and sleeping in your car at that? And why do you have all this junk food in here? This crap will catch up with you one day. Trust me, I know." He said, tugging on his plump round belly. He was right. Dahlia lived off super donuts, lunchroom cookies, Funyuns, and water. It didn't make much of a difference to her because it was what she could afford at the time.

"Mr. Jones, I am here to see my grandmother. You know that, cut me some slack."

"The slack I'm cutting you has me hanging on to my job by a thread. I get chewed out every morning that the director comes here and sees your car parked here. I cannot continue to lie for you, especially when you get careless and park in the handicapped zone."

"Okay, I'll move it today. I promise." As soon as he walked back into the building, Dahlia grabbed her travel kit, clean underwear, and a hairbrush. She had been living in her car for at least six months. Everything she owned, which was not much, was in the car. She did her best to keep it clean and organized since it was so small. Toiletries were in the glove compartment while all the snacks covered the passenger floor and seat. She kept her duffle bag in the backseat because she used it as a pillow. The only thing that could fit in the trunk was the spare tire and a bin with important papers and old photos.

Dahlia headed into the nursing home as she did every morning. "I'm here to see Daisy Greene. And before you say anything, I know visiting hours isn't for another two hours, but I have to be at work in thirty minutes. By the time I get off, there won't be any more visiting hours." She said in a rush.

"Slow down, Ms. Greene. I swear you're always in such a rush. You're too young and pretty to wear that stress on your face like that. And have you eaten? Here take this." She said, handing her a bagel and visitors' sticker to see her grandmother.

"Thanks so much! I owe you!" Dahlia ran down the hall and detoured to one of the bathrooms before stopping in to see her granny. Dahlia's routine was bulletproof. She would sleep in her car parked outside the nursing home, wake up, shower, brush her teeth, then head to see her grandma. From there, she walked to work which was conveniently three blocks down the street. Although Dahlia was dealt a shitty hand, she kept a poker face. She never really had much, so living out of her car didn't bother her as most people would have thought it would.

She entered her grandmother's room. To no surprise, she lay there looking at the ceiling with her eyes open as she had been for the past six months, hooked up to a ventilator. Dahlia brushed her hair and massaged her feet with lotion like she usually did. She told her about her morning so far and told her the plans for the rest of the day. Each time, Dahlia hoped and waited for her to respond back. But she never did.

Before she left, she recited the same line she always did. "Hey, grandma. You're gonna get through this, okay. Promise me that." Dahlia kissed her on her forehead and left her room.

On her way out, she was stopped by the director.

"Ms. Greene. Do you have a moment?"

"I'm actually running late for work. Can we talk later?" He completely ignored what she just said and continued anyway.

"Ms. Greene, I'm sure you could appreciate how accommodating we have been. You're a couple of months behind on your payment, but that's not what I wanted to talk to you about. Your grandmother is not progressing, and we would like to talk to you about hospice. She could stay here, we would continue to keep her comfortable, and she wouldn't be in any pain. But Ms. Greene, we aren't doing anything for her, and frankly speaking, she is holding a bed. A bed for someone that could benefit from the care we give."

"As I said, I'm late for work." Dahlia rushed out of the facility and threw her toiletries bag in the car. She grabbed her phone out of the armrest and jetted to the diner. Dahlia was beyond annoyed that Mr. Lieberman kept shoving hospice down her throat. *My granny just needed some time. That's it, just a little more time,* she thought to herself.

It was only 8:30 am and Dahlia was already heading over to her fifth table of the morning. A beautiful middle-aged woman with honey-colored skin and silky, luxurious hair sat there scrolling on the latest iPhone. "Can I help you? Have you had enough time to look at the menu?" Dahlia asked.

"Not really, so what do you recommend?" She replied.

"Well, the tea cake is crappy, and the croissants are dry. The best cook doesn't get here until 12. You would be better off getting a cup of coffee and calling it a day."

"Okay, I'll take a cup of coffee, six creams, and four sugars," she replied.

"Alright, coming right up." Dahlia headed to the counter to pour her coffee. This woman had been in here every day this week and never ordered anything. Dahlia was pretty sure she would not order anything today either, but to her surprise, she did. Although she had only exchanged a few words with the stranger, she envied her. In that short exchange, Dahlia noted the diamonds in her ears and how perfectly manicured her nails appeared, compared to how chipped and uneven Dahlia's were. Each day, her perfume lingered long after she left the diner. She wore Creed, and that was easily a thousand dollars a bottle. *So, what the hell was she doing in here, patronizing this hole in the wall?*

"Here you go, ma'am, one coffee, six creams, four sugars. Can I get you anything else?"

"How long are you going to work in this diner?" She asked. The woman waved her hand, inviting Dahlia to sit with her.

"Excuse me?" She asked, intrigued.

"With those eyes, that jawline, and that dark chocolate complexion, you could be making a lot more money. I can help you make that happen."

"Thank You." Dahlia blushed. "I barely make enough to get by. The jobs I want to work for require crisp white shirts and pencil skirts for their interviews, and I can't afford that. If I can't come correct, I won't come at all. So, I don't know. Are you a modeling scout or something?"

"Modeling scout? No, but I am in the business of... let's say providing customer service."

"Well, can you give me more information about the position? That is if you have an opening for what you do."

"I have already told you everything you need to know. Either you want the position, or you don't." She stated.

"Listen, you came to me. I am not looking for any handouts from you or nobody else. I cannot just agree to work for you without knowing what it is you do exactly."

Dahlia watched as the beautiful woman applied an extra coat of lipstick, which was pointless because she never touched her coffee. She slid her glasses down from her forehead and placed her purse in front of her. "Well, Dahlia," she said, glancing at her name tag, "you should get back to work. Finish bussing these tables. If you really do not care or aren't even a little curious at how I can change your life, go back to sleeping in your 1996 Sunfire and beg Sweet Baby Jesus that this weather goes easy on you. We all know how rough a Chicago winter could be. You could have any job you want. Don't give me that bullshit about not having a nice interview shirt or pants to wear. The Goodwill has attire for less than five dollars; you can afford that. You just don't want to work- a traditional job, that is. You don't want to clock eight hours every day only to bring home a check that can't fill up your tank and buy you a pair of shoes. I got the solution you're looking for. It is not my fault if you don't have the balls to go for it."

Dahlia stared at the woman who pretty much told her to have several seats. "Why me?"

"I have had my eyes on you for quite some time, Dahlia. You remind me a lot of myself. Beautiful, feisty, honest, and most importantly, efficient. I can put you on, and I don't have to worry about you fucking up my money."

"Okay, can you please just tell me what it is that you do? I can't agree to something without having the full story." The woman pulled out a wad of money and placed a $100 bill on the table. She wrote something on it and slid it to Dahlia across the table.

"Meet me here. I can show you better than I can tell you." She eyed the red bottoms on the woman's feet as she walked out of the door. Dahlia stuffed the bill into her back pocket and continued the rest of her shift.

That evening, Dahlia stared at the hundred-dollar bill all the way back to her car. *If I had any sense, I would use that money to get some decent interview clothes, buy myself something to eat, and put some gas in my car so I could use the heat and stop freezing every night. But if I were smart, I'd say fuck everything else and meet her at the address listed on it because I am sure there was more where it came from.* Dahlia put the bill back into her back pocket and sprinted the rest of the way to the nursing home.

When she got there, Dahlia's car was being lifted onto a tow truck. "Wait, wait, wait!" She yelled as she ran towards the tow truck. "This is my car! What are you doing?"

"I'm taking it to the lot." He said, smacking his gum.

"But I am here now. Can I just move it?" She pleaded.

"Hell no, lady, you got tickets piled up, and you're in a handicapped spot. The city does not play when it comes to these tickets. They'll usually give you a boot, but since it's private property, I guess the owner of this spot gave permission to tow it."

"Okay, wait. I got one hundred dollars. If I give you that, can you give me my car back?"

"Let me spell it out for you. The CITY OF CHICAGO OWNS YOUR CAR NOW. You'll have to get these tickets paid in order to get it back. I'm just the messenger." He attempted to get in his truck before she grabbed his arm with one final plea.

"Sir, can I at least get my stuff out? Everything I own is in this car. Please?"

"You tell me what you need out of it, and I'll get it." He replied. "How did you get this far owing $5,000 in tickets anyway?"

After giving Dahlia her items, he drove off. She stood outside the nursing home looking dumber than she did before she left this morning. The chill was in the air, and Dahlia started to feel her toes starting to go numb. Visiting hours were over. It was a little after five, and Dahlia had nowhere to sleep for the night. She wanted to slap the shit out of Mr. Lieberman. She knew his fat petty ass did this because she blew him off this morning. It was the middle of March in Chicago which means you could expect rain or a snowstorm. Either way, being without shelter was a death wish. Because, if the weather didn't get you, a stray bullet could. Just then, Dahlia remembered she did, in fact, have somewhere to go. She just needed to find a way to get there.

Chapter Two

The bus dropped Dahlia off at the end of what she thought was a deserted block. She passed a few houses on her way down the quiet street. Exhausted from the day's events, Dahlia was just about ready to give up until she crossed some train tracks and ended up in front of a huge building. *This couldn't be the right address.* It looked like an ordinary building on the outside, run down and even abandoned. But still, she truly had nothing to lose. Her stomach was in knots as she headed to the huge metal door and rang the bell.

"Can I help you?" Dahlia heard a voice say. She read what was on the hundred-dollar bill the lady gave her.

"Um, uh, sugar, spice, and everything nice." She said nervously. The large metal door glided open and Dahlia hesitantly entered.

While the outside looked like something in the middle of a horror movie, the inside was a different story. It was beautiful. Dahlia looked around in awe at the floor-to-ceiling windows, beautiful dark oak wood floors, modern décor, and the scent of lavender filled the air. The ambiance was finished with Japanese folk music. It was weird but right up her alley.

"What's your name, ma'am?" A girl at the front glass desk asked her.

"I'm Dahlia." The girl nodded while picking up her desk phone to inform whoever was on the other end that Dahlia had just arrived. After placing the phone back on the receiver, she smiled.

"We have been expecting you. Right this way." Dahlia followed the lady up the iron staircase, carefully holding on to the railing, which appeared to separate at least three floors.

There were lots of girls there—Dahlia counted at least 16—of all different shades of melanin. Some of the girls were gorgeous, others not so much, but their bodies made up for what their faces lacked.

"Where are the Suga Babies? Bring them to me", the beautiful woman from the diner called out. "I'm Charmaine," she said, officially introducing herself. "I want you to meet a few people." Dahlia was still dumbfounded. It didn't register to her what was happening because she was in awe of the fast-paced environment. It reminded her of a scene from Showgirls. Nevertheless, no sooner than Charmaine made the request, three girls appeared before her.

"Dahlia, this is Lux, Keena, and Naima. Girls, this is Dahlia, our new Suga Baby."

"Dahlia, what kind of name is that?" Keena giggled.

"My grandmother loves flowers, so she named me after her favorite one." Dahlia replied, trying not to sound offended.

"Yeah, Keena is right. Dahlia is a *dated* name. We're going to call you Lia." Charmaine added. Dahlia was both impressed and irritated by Charmaine's boldness.

"We don't need no new girls up in here, especially if they gon be scary and fuckin up the money like last one." Lux rolled her eyes.

"Simmer down Lux, you don't call no mother fuckin shots around here. I've told you countless times about your smart-ass mouth. Focus on the money you are NOT bringing in and step your game up before I put your prissy ass in the clubs with them level 1 girls." Charmaine spat. Dahlia didn't know what any of that meant, but that shut the Lux girl right up.

"Okay Lia, we have a big event tonight, and it's your debut. The girls can take you on a quick tour, show you your room, then Dru can get you ready."

"My room?" Until that very moment, Dahlia had forgotten that she didn't have anywhere to sleep due to her car being towed a couple hours earlier. "Like, my own room?"

"Yes, your room, unless you prefer to go back to your car. I'm pretty sure you don't."

I couldn't if I wanted to, she thought to herself.

"She's pretty," Naima said, and Keena nodded her head in agreement. "Come on, Lia, let us show you around."

"Hurry up!" Charmaine shouted. "I want her in hair and makeup in thirty minutes. She's starting tonight." Charmaine disappeared into the sea of women, while Lia trailed behind her new co-workers.

"Okay Lia, so do you remember where you came in?" Naima asked.

"Yes, the lobby, I guess. It had two elevators, one on each side, a beautiful mural on the brick wall, and a glass desk. There was a dark-skinned girl sitting there; I'm assuming she's a receptionist?"

"Um, okkayy, I wasn't asking you to memorize it." She laughed. "But it is impressive that you did. Anyway, I asked you that because the woman sitting at the desk's name is Taylor. You go to her for anything you need. Whether it's towels, bedding, or reporting an incident, you go to her. She's Charmaine's right hand—you never talk to Char directly, unless she requests you. You go to Taylor first."

"Okay, got it, holla at the receptionist if I need anything."

"Girl, stop calling Taylor a receptionist. I think she's an ex-Taekwondo fighter or something. She doesn't play. I have watched her throw bitches all around this place. She is small, but don't let her looks fool you. Which brings me to rule number one. Never judge a book by its cover. Do not make it a habit to go for the obvious guy. They'll all look sharp; we know they have money, or else we wouldn't be in the same space as them. You want to make sure whoever you pull in has no issue spending the money they do have on you. You do whatever it takes to make sure they will keep coming back for more." Naima emphasized. The girls continued to walk until they got to level one.

"Alright, this is level one. The level one girls work in Chars' strip club. They are at the bottom of the barrel."

"Excuse me!" Keena blurted out. "I'm not a bottom-of-the-barrel bitch! Get that shit right!"

"Oh girl, please, calm down. I mean as far as the business goes."

"Well, be clear! Shit! Don't do me. When I was a level one girl, we had a smooth little system. Just because we were dancing doesn't mean we weren't worthy."

"Relax, if you like being a level one girl so much, then you might as well go back to being one," Naima said.

"Well, let's not take it that far now." Keena laughed.

"Exactly, come on y'all." The three girls headed up to level 2. "Ok, so these girls I don't know much about, and Charmaine likes to keep it that way. They only socialize with each other and are rarely seen. It's only about seven of them. Over there is Jesse. She's pretty much in charge of them and is the only one who reports directly to Charmaine. There's one person from each level that reports to Char, and for us, that would be Lux."

"How many levels are there?" Dahlia asked

"Three." Naima responded while checking her phone to see what the time was.

"So, what is the third level? You only showed me two?" Dahlia asked curiously.

"The Suga Babies. Me, Naima, Lux, and now you. She only keeps four at a time, never less, never more. While them other bitches chipping nails and shaking ass to get their money, all we got to do is dress up, be arm candy, and good company."

"How much money do we make?" Dahlia was intrigued.

"I can make three stacks in like four to eight hours," Keena interjected. Naima agreed.

Dahlia spit her drink out, nearly choking on it. "Three thousand dollars in four hours?! Doing what exactly?"

"Whew, girl, you not that bright, are you? Charmaine puts us in a room of young or older professionals, and we show them a good time. Whatever they want, they get. Frankly speaking, they get you." Naima smiled.

"I don't know if I like the way that sounds. This is clearly not a gig for me. I don't sleep around; I don't give a damn how much money you put in front of me."

"I didn't say anything about sleeping around. We're not escorts, and Charmaine will be the first to tell you that. But, if one of those suit and tie niggas wanna throw a couple of bands my way for sex, I'm down."

"Bitches be in relationships fuckin for free anyway." Keena blurted out. "You can act all high and mighty if you want to, but I'mma get paid," she continued.

"Well, if you do decide to go that route, do not let Charmaine find out; she'll tell you in a minute that she ain't running a hoe house. You'll be gone quicker than you start."

The girls headed to the final level of the large warehouse, which was much quieter than the other two. Dahlia's brain was filled with many questions but no reservations. This was indeed a job she could get used to. Especially if it didn't include her degrading herself. But still, anyone could admit it sounded too good to be true, so Dahlia asked more questions.

"Naima, if you can bring home thousands in a few hours, why are you still in the business, or why don't you have your own place to stay at the least?"

"Charmaine takes a cut of whatever we earn. You'll see the breakdown of everything in your contract. As far as living here, we pay for the rooms we sleep in, but not much else. The only thing we really pay for is clothes. That's it."

"Do we have to stay here if we do not want to?"

"Good question, but I don't really know how to answer that. I don't see why you wouldn't want to. You'll be paying three hundred dollars a month. You do not have to pay for water, gas, electricity, or food. It's a stain." Naima said.

"Yeah, you are right; that is pretty decent." Dahlia remarked.

"Alright, here's your room. Keena is next to you. Me and Lux are across from you. Take a few moments to look around, hop in the shower then you need to go back to the second floor to get your hair and stuff done. Charmaine said there's a gig tonight."

"Okay, I have a question."

Naima let out an exasperated sigh. "Of course, you do; you're so inquisitive. What is it now?"

"You only named one rule. Are there any others?" Dahlia asked.

"Yeah, don't fall in love...with anybody. Client or outside niggas is a hell to the no. And don't ask me any more questions. You wore me out." She laughed.

Naima retired to her room, as did Keena. Before Dahlia headed into her room, she saw Lux, who turned her nose up at her before slamming her door. One thing Dahlia avoided was unnecessary drama. Dahlia refused to feed into whatever issues Lux had with her. She assumed that Lux was not receptive to new girls. It was a shame Lux's attitude was so stank because she was gorgeous. Her light brown skin, long locs, and almond-shaped eyes couldn't hide how ugly she was on the inside.

"Girl Bye," Dahlia said aloud and closed her room door.

Dahlia glanced around her room. Not gonna lie; it was better than anything she'd ever had. In the past, Dahlia slept on dingy mattresses, piss-stained carpet, and, at times, bare wooden floors that creaked with the slightest of movement before she went to live with her grandmother. But even then, she shared a bed with her granny in a one-bedroom apartment.

The Pastel peach walls and the cream-colored carpet were simply fine with Dahlia, who finally had a place to call her own. The room looked like a mini studio, and she was more than happy to reside in it. After unpacking her small duffle bag, the only item to her name, she got in the shower and nearly lost track of time. Dahlia hurried downstairs to Dru and introduced herself. He applied her makeup and picked out a nice little black dress for her to wear. At about 6:30, Charmaine came to escort Dahlia, Naima, Keena, and Lux to the car.

Dahlia was quiet the entire limo ride to the location. Many thoughts surrounding her new lifestyle clouded her head. Explanation of the different levels, how nice the room Charmaine assigned her was, how bitchy Lux is and what the hell she was getting herself into, just to name a few. All money's not good money, but it seemed like the girls were happy, healthy, and complaint-free. Dahlia was ready to dive in headfirst, of course, because she had goals, and only money could get her there.

Dahlia, the girls, and her new boss pulled up to the Signature Room at the 95th. The name was strange, but it was an upscale spot, with breathtaking views of the city and the classiest cocktails. Dahlia pretended to look the other way when Lux took two sniffs of coke, followed by Keena and Naima throwing back shots. Charmaine dabbed herself with perfume and they all got out of the limo before heading into the building. Char was greeted by name by every single staff member, from the owner down to the custodial engineer.

The elevator ride seemed long as Dahlia anticipated what was before her. Her thoughts were interrupted by Char's voice. "Alright, girls, be available, make a good impression, make me look good, and let's get this money." The elevator opened to the 95th floor, and the fivesome walked out and into a room full of nothing but men with a handful of other women. Keena, Naima, and Lux immediately disappeared into the crowd, leaving Dahlia looking like a bump on a log. Her feet were stuck to the floor and she had a fear of lump in her throat. She didn't know what to do. Char caught her eyes from across the room and nodded her head at Lia, seemingly telling her to go mingle. Lia was approached by a server who offered her some champagne. Lia downed two glasses then found her first target.

As the night went on, Lia was offered drinks from several guys, but she made sure to pace herself. She observed Keena leaving with a handsome short guy. *Dammit, if I don't step my game up, I will go home empty-handed.* Just then, Charmaine approached and introduced Lia to the pleasantly plump bald white guy.

"Lia, this is Mr. Packonowski. He's the CEO of a printing company." Mr. Pacanowski kissed Lia's hand and greeted her. She indulged him in conversation for what seemed like an hour until he excused himself. He went to talk to Charmaine, and Lia just knew he was complaining about her. He was probably telling Charmaine that Lia was dull and uninteresting, and hell, she probably was. *Why did I have to get stuck with the chubby Italian soprano wannabe,* she thought.

Mr. Pacanowski left the event while Charmaine summoned Lia. "Here's the key card to Mr. Paconowski's room. Meet him there in twenty minutes."

"Oh hell no." she spat.

"What's the problem?" Charmaine asked.

"Charmaine, I'm not about to screw that fat ass white man." She immediately covered her mouth, realizing she was still speaking to her boss.

"Listen, little girl. When you're in a position that requires direct customer service, you have to put on your poker face. Now you're new to all this, but I'm not. I've known Mr. Paconowski for years; he's harmless. Don't disrespect him. And trust me, having sex is the LAST thing on his mind."

"So, what does he want?"

She laughed hysterically; you'll see.

Chapter Three

Dahlia entered Mr. Paconowski's suite and found him dressed down to a robe. His suite was larger than any apartment she shared with her grandmother as well as more glamorous. From the plush carpet to the view of the city skyline and the gold finishes, Dahlia concluded that the room was at least one grand a night. She was taken aback because he had soft music playing and a bottle of champagne in a bucket.

"Don't be shy, sweetheart. Can I get you a glass of champagne?" He asked.

"Sure," she replied. She figured she would need something to take the edge off in this uncomfortable situation she found herself in. Dahlia was clear on what she was willing to do, and screwing an oversized white man wasn't on her list. Mr. Paconowski proceeded to ask her questions about her childhood, which she lied about, amongst other things. "What's on your mind for this evening?" She whispered.

Mr. Paconowski guided her to the chaise next to the window and instructed her to take her shoes off. He pulled up a chair and sat in front of her. He grabbed

Dahlia's foot with his chubby sausage hands and massaged it. Without warning, he slipped her toe into his mouth. Dahlia was taken by surprise, and she immediately yanked away, but that only sent him into a frenzy. He devoured her foot further. Licking between each of her toes, gnawing on her foot, and, without warning, he started jacking off. Moments later, Mr. Paconowski turned red, grunted, and exploded. He lay there panting heavily while Dahlia sat in bewilderment, trying to hold back her disgust and a little bit of laughter.

Later, he gathered himself, wiped his genitalia off, and closed his robe. After washing his hands, he opened the safe next to his bed and pulled out a stack of cash. "One, two, three." He counted. "There, one thousand. When can I see you again?"

"Thank you, baby." Dahlia replied, trying to stay calm. "Just let Charmaine know. She'll get in contact with me." He kissed her hand, and she exited the room.

Dahlia was cheesing extra hard because she definitely didn't expect a stack, especially for letting him suck on her toes. "This is going to be easy money," she said aloud. Dahlia headed to the grand room, where she'd initially met Mr. Paconowski, and found Charmaine and the rest of the girls waiting for her.

"How was it?" Charmaine teased, trying to contain her laughter.

"Piece of cake. How much do I owe you?"

"Pocket it for now. Tomorrow morning we'll discuss expenses and contracts. You did good tonight." Charmaine replied.

Before heading back to the compound, the girls and their boss stopped to pick up food. Dahlia indulged in her pizza puff and fries with mild sauce. Then she finished it off with a peach Crush pop. Dahlia slept like a baby for the first time in half a year. She had a full stomach, a couple of bills in her purse, and she was able to sleep with the security of not wondering if someone was going to break into her car with her in it.

The next morning, Dahlia met with Charmaine. Her beautiful office was glass, with pink finishes. She sat down and waited in silence, admiring everything that was before her. Charmaine handed Dahlia three pieces of paper and asked her to read over them. Dahlia glanced at everything from the rules of the position and the rules as far as housing goes. She honed in on the percentage of the earnings she would owe to Charmaine.

"Do you have any questions, Lia?" Charmaine asked, finally breaking the silence.

"Yeah, just a couple. Do you take 30% of my earnings, no matter how much I make? And Naima mentioned 'no falling in love'?"

"That is absolutely correct. I cannot have any jealous boyfriends, or girlfriends in some cases, messing up my cash flow. That goes for your clients as well. You need to keep them at a distance. They need to know that you have boundaries and respecting them is non-negotiable. Nobody gets special treatment--this is a business. And as far as the percentage, that's right. Whether you make $300, or $3,000, I still take thirty percent."

"Okay, I don't have any other questions." Dahlia took a pink feathery pen from her desk and gladly signed her name. She handed the papers to Charmaine, who sat with a big smile on her face.

"Well, if there is nothing else, welcome. Make yourself at home and stay focused on the money." She said, extending her hand to her new employee. Dahlia shook her hand, smiled, and exited her office.

Dahlia had five steady clients within three months, which grossed her at least $6,000 each month. Paco's foot fetish was an easy thousand. Then there was Mr. Williams. He was easy money as well. All Dahlia had to do was listen to him complain about his wife and how she lacks in her duties around their home- easy five hundred dollars. But then she had clients like Foxy. She was a married mother of three and her only female client. She loved to role play and often wanted Dahlia to give her massages and *accidentally* slip her fingers into her essence until she was satisfied. Then she requested to suck her own juices off them. The weirdest shit ever, but if she liked it, Dahlia loved it-- especially since it was another stack in it for her. Dahlia's last two clients required a little more work. They were businessmen, and she enjoyed working with them the most. There was nothing intimate involved. Instead, she was required to attend business dinners with them, pose as their girlfriend and make small talk with their clients to help close their deals. Mr. Phillips and Mr. Howard paid her $1,500 apiece.

After paying Charmaine her portions, buying clothes, and covering her room and board, Dahlia was able to save about $10,000 within three months. That wasn't bad.

Dahlia was so consumed by her new lifestyle that she had completely neglected to take care of business and had not been to visit her grandmother. Last time she saw her was before she started working with Charmaine. Dahlia had not even called the facility to check in on her. She had no clients for the weekend and thought it would be the perfect time to drop in on her grandmother. Keena rented a car for the weekend since she had errands of her own to run. Charmaine said she was going out of town, so there were no new events. Instead, they were to continue entertaining their current clients if they called. Dahlia asked Keena to take her to the nursing home on her way to the city. When she got there, she anxiously hopped out of the car, excited to see her granny.

"Hey, Mr. Lieberman. I know it has been a while since I visited and at least a month since we last spoke, but I'm here today. I got $5,000. That should cover a little of the bill I owe. How is she doing?"

"Oh, hey Ms. Greene, no need for the money. Medicaid finally kicked in, and the bill was settled a couple weeks ago. Unfortunately, your grandmother passed on shortly after."

"What the hell do you mean she passed on? I didn't withdraw care. Nobody contacted me! How fuckin dare you all?" Dahlia hauled off and jumped on Mr. Lieberman. The security guard and nurse used all their strength to get her away from him.

"This is a business, Ms. Greene." He said, adjusting his tie. "You signed the do not resuscitate paperwork. She coded while we were trying to trach and peg her. We called you several times, Ms. Greene."

"You fat, funky muthafucka! I'mma beat yo ass!" She continued to yell. "I'mma get this piece of shit shut down. You wanted my grandmother out of here anyway!"

"Escort her out of here." Dahlia heard him say as they dragged her down the hall.

She hopped in the car with Keena and cried her eyes away. When they arrived back at the warehouse, Charmaine's security was loading her car. She saw the look in Dahlia's eyes and led her into her office. She explained the situation to Char, bawling away, and Char just stared at her.

"It just seems wrong to end care without contacting family. This hurts so much." Dahlia continued.

"Lia, you've been here for a while. I have rarely heard you mention your grandmother. Are you sure it is not guilt that is consuming you?"

"What the hell, Char! Is this your way of comforting me? I'm not guilty! I have been the only person there for my grandmother for the past 22 years! Nobody had the right to take her from me. I don't give a fuck who it is."

"And you don't have the right to keep her around just because you are afraid to let her go. It's not fair to her, and it is not fair to you, Lia. Your grandmother is in a much better place. It will hurt a while, but you'll be okay. Take some time for yourself while I'm away this weekend. Get it together and regroup. When I get back, we are back to the money."

"Maybe money brings you happiness, and that's why it's so easy for you to dismiss my feelings regarding the only mother figure I've ever had. It's all good. You clearly don't have kids, or else you wouldn't have just said that dumb shit to me."

Charmaine smiled on the inside because Dahlia had the fire that she needed for her organization. She'd never let her know she admired her feistiness, so she checked her instead. "Lil girl, you're grieving, so I'mma let that language and tone slide for now. Don't let it happen again.

Dahlia nodded and stormed out of the office.

Chapter Four

Lux knelt on the ground with her tongue hanging out of her mouth. She made heavy panting sounds as if she was a dog. She often pretended to be one because that is what he wanted her to do. Her most important client was Black Greystone. He was an oil tycoon and managed to slip under Char's radar, thankfully for Lux. He was the wealthiest client on the elite list, and every time he came into town, Lux was the first person he called.

"BEG!" His deep voice commanded. On cue, Lux began to beg. "Please, oh please, zaddy, let me make you feel good." She whimpered. He removed his boxers and commanded Lux to come to him. Slowly, she crawled over on all fours. Licking her lips, she looked up at him with innocent eyes awaiting his next instruction. "Open wide." He demanded. Lux opened her mouth, ready to go to work. Black was an extremely attractive older man, most definitely. His body was on point, his muscles were stacked, and his caramel skin stood out against his salt and pepper beard. While his pipe made her weak in the knees, it wasn't his dick that had her salivating; it was those ten stacks she knew he would drop on her at the end of his trip. "GO," he said. Lux relaxed her throat and slid her lips over his member. She slurped sloppily and deep-throated him multiple times, watching the sweat gather on his bald head. Black's muscles began to tense as he gripped her head and slammed into her mouth further. His nut built, and she gladly allowed his lust to shower her face.

Black demanded that Lux join him in the shower for round two, and she quickly obliged. After they finished their steamy exchange in the shower, he got dressed. He had several business meetings for the day and needed to start them as soon as possible. Lux dried her body off and put on the robe from the hotel's linen closet. She was grateful he was in town, but she was already exhausted. She'd been catering to his needs since his flight got in yesterday evening. Now here it was morning and she jumped for joy on the inside knowing he'd be heading out for his work day, giving her some time to recuperate.

"I want some more girls in here. Didn't Charmaine just hire somebody else?" He asked, placing his watch on his wrist and adjusting his cufflinks. Lux hesitated before answering. One thing she hated was to share her money, but she knew Black's thirst needed to be quenched, and she couldn't do it alone. The last time she selfishly tried to have him for herself, she walked with a limp for a few days.

"Yeah, she did, but I don't really know her like that. I can bring Keena." She suggested, hoping he would agree.

"I want the new girl. Keena can come, too, but I most definitely want to see the new girl. The menu is next to the phone. Order whatever you want; I'mma stop back in here for lunch. Have my pussy ready for me when I get back." Black stated. Lux allowed her sugar daddy to kiss her on the forehead before he left the room. She cuddled in the massive king-sized bed and ordered up some waffles with whipped cream. While she indulged in her meal, she thought about the best way to rope in Dahlia. She did not know her well and could not trust if she would be willing to go behind Char's back to meet the Elite list of clients. More importantly, she didn't know if she would be willing to submit to Black's appetite. Nevertheless, she needed to find a way to get her on board. Black was her ticket out of this lifestyle, and she planned to do everything to make and *keep* him happy.

Lux slept like a baby after Black came back to the room around twelve thirty to dick her down further. Upon rising, she remembered she had to return to the compound to check on the girls since Char was off on her business trip. Since she'd been with Char the longest, Char gave her the responsibility of being in charge of the girls, and she humbly accepted it. Char didn't trust just anybody so Lux made sure she dotted all of her I's and crossed her T's, hoping not to fuck up.

***

Dahlia preferred to be in her room sulking and sobbing over the death of her grandmother, but instead, she was forced into some underground party that Lux was throwing. Apparently, whenever Charmaine went out of town, the girls contacted Char's elite list of clients and met up with them. Dahlia was surprised to be invited at all, seeing as though Lux had not said more than five words since she started working with them. But today, Lux offered her condolences about her loved one and told her she could help her take her mind off it, giving her the rundown on the party.

The small event was held at the Nobu Hotel in downtown Chicago, mainly because Black always stayed there. The four girls were expected to entertain a group of ten men and, depending on what they wanted, the payout could be at least three thousand apiece. Now sure, these girls made more than that at Charmaine's other parties, but this money would be tax-free- or Charmaine free, that is. Since she knew nothing about it, she couldn't take a cut, and that was what kept Naima and Keena tight-lipped about Lux's side operation.

Dahlia sat at the bar, away from the other girls. She noticed herself sinking into a slight depression when she suddenly felt a splash of something on her feet.

"Damn, watch where the hell you're going." She blurted out. Whoever this clumsy nigga was just made her release the last bit of patience she had left, especially with all she had been through lately.

"My bad lil mama, can we get a clean rag over here?" She heard the deep voice say. Dahlia took her stiletto off and sat back on the red barstool. She listened to his voice rambling on but was too fixated on her shoe to make out the words. She examined her shoes closely, hoping they weren't ruined.

"What's your name, lady?"

"Lia." She said without looking up.

"Lia. I like it. Is that short for something?"

"Look, you have already messed up my shoe. What else do you want? I don't have time for the unnecessary small talk." She said, finally looking up into the stranger's eyes, and she was glad she did. This dude had mesmerizing eyes and a full beard and goatee that sat perfectly against his Hershey skin. She studied him from head to toe. He was perfect, from his smile with sparkling white teeth; his muscles that were semi hidden under his suit and his fade that was finished with a knot brush. "I apologize; forgive my rudeness. This week has not been friendly to me. It's just Lia for now, and you are?" She said, finally smiling and extending her hand.

"It's all good; no need to apologize. I'm the one in the wrong here. The name is Lenox." He extended his hand to shake hers and motioned toward the bartender with his free hand, then leaned against the bar in front of her. She observed him closely. He appeared out of place. He *could* fit into the clientele, but then again, he didn't. He was smooth but a little rough around the edges as well. She had never seen him before, which was not necessarily unusual, considering this was her first time at one of the underground parties thrown by the girls. Although she was pretty observant, Charmaine taught her to pick up on the most subtle details when pulling in a new client. She told her to pay attention to their mannerisms, scent, attire, and, most importantly, what they drink. "I'll have a cognac neat and for the lady--"

"Vodka Tonic and bring Mr. Lenox an ashtray and cigar cutter." She added.

"What makes you think I need an ashtray and cigar cutter?" He questioned intriguingly.

"Your drink suggests you've had a long day and you're ready to take a load off. You've eyed the young lady at the end of the bar a few times. It's not that you are attracted to her. It's because you're admiring the sense of relief she's seemingly experiencing, smoking her Juul. You're waiting on your drink, so you can take a cigar out of your pocket and join in on that relief."

"Are you the law or something?" He laughed while taking the cigar out of his pocket.

"No, I just know men." She took a sip of her drink that was placed in front of her and handed him the cigar cutter. "So, tell me about yourself. What do you do for a living?" Lia asked.

"Why is it that women immediately ask what men do for a living? How about you tell me what you do for a living?"

"Because we want to make sure y'all can take care of us before we waste our time." She laughed. "I'm in customer service--image consulting, you could say."

"That's interesting. Could you elaborate?"

"Nothing much to elaborate on. It's simple, I make men like you look good. That's why you're here, right?" He looked completely dumbfounded, which piqued her curiosity more. It was clear he wasn't on Lux's elite clientele list.

"Actually, I'm meeting some folks here for a special event. And now it looks like they are ready to go." He said, noticing one of his boys waving to get his attention. "I would apologize for bumping into you, but then I wouldn't have the opportunity to ask you for your number. I would love to take you out and get to know you better." Dahlia hesitated for many reasons. For one, she knew she didn't want him to become a client, and two, it appeared he had no intention of becoming one.

"I don't know you like that, Lenox. Besides, I'm sure we'll never see each other again after this day. So, let's just call it what it is, a chance encounter. Enjoy your night." She smiled.

"Until we meet again, sexy—because we *will*." He said, kissing her hand before leaving with his friends. Dahlia got lost in her thoughts about the handsome stranger. He was very attractive, and Dahlia knew that would mean he could bring her nothing but trouble, especially considering the no dating rule. But still, there was something about him. Dahlia was snapped out of her daydream by Lux and an older gentleman.

"Lia. LIA! Pay attention, girl. This is Mr. Greystone. He asked to be introduced to you."

"Hello, Mr. Greystone," she said, flirting with her eyes. He grabbed her hand and kissed it.

"Charmed," he replied. "I'm having a small party back in my room. I want you to join us." Dahlia looked at Keena and Lux, who practically begged her to say yes with their eyes.

"Sure, Mr. Greystone, I'd love to join you all." Dahlia agreed.

The elevator ride to Mr. Greystone's suite was both awkward and uncomfortable. Keena held on to his arm while Lux placed kisses on his neck. Dahlia stood awkwardly in the opposite corner of the elevator while Mr. Greystone eyed her lasciviously. They entered his suite. Lux poured four glasses of chilled champagne that was waiting in the ice bucket and offered each of them a glass. Keena brought out the powder, and both she and Lux indulged before offering Dahlia some. Dahlia declined their offer as Lux turned the Bluetooth speaker on and sat Black in the chair. Keena swayed her slim waist, plump ass, and extra curvy hips in front of Black slowly to the music. Lux joined her, caressing her body. Shortly after, Lux and Keena began to kiss and fondle each other. Dahlia looked at them in disbelief and took that as her sign to leave the suite. She took her champagne to the head and excused herself from the trois.

Her heart throbbed as she stood alone on the elevator. She hoped her Uber she'd reserved on the way out of the room would be waiting for her by the time she got down to the lobby. On her way out, she ran into Lenox, and though she tried to avoid his gaze, he called out to her.

"Lia! Let me guess, you thought twice about giving me your number, so you're here to do that now?" He asked jogging over to her.

"You guessed wrong, I am waiting for my Uber."

"What's a fine ass woman like you doing waiting on an Uber? Let me take you home?"

"Boy, I don't know you," she smiled.

"So, let's change that." He took her phone out of her hand, then dialed and saved his number in it. "Now you got my number, and if you don't use it within 72 hours, I'll take that personally and call you myself. You say we don't know each other, now we have the opportunity." He said.

"Yo, we out," someone called out. Lenox looked up, nodded his head, and said his goodbye to Dahlia.

Dahlia took the lengthy uber ride back to the compound in the southwest suburbs. This had been the longest day of her life. Though it started with her finding out her grandmother was dead, it ended with her being enticed by a handsome stranger. When she got back to the compound, she took a long bath and settled into bed. Before drifting off to sleep, she did something she knew she probably shouldn't have done. She texted Lenox.

Chapter Five

Lenox rose every day at the same time each morning- 5am. His daily routine consisted of meditating, journaling then exercising. Method Man's "You're All I Need" looped on repeat and filled his studio condo as he prepared himself for his daily workout routine.

Lenox sat on his workout bench and began pressing one hundred fifty pounds. He paused periodically to sip from his water bottle, then continued to press more. After a few reps, he went over to his punching bag and started his kickboxing sequence. Working out usually offered Lenox a piece of mind, but today he seemed a little off. Meeting that fiery girl at the hotel consumed him, as did his thoughts regarding his sister.

Lenox blended his peanut butter and banana protein smoothie and transferred it to a glass. Sipping the smoothie, Lenox headed over to his bookshelf and peeked into the journal that he kept his notes in. He looked at all the tips and clues he gathered regarding his sister. He noted the last date he actually spoke to her and the last day she was physically seen.

 Every now and then, when he would call her, she'd send him to voicemail but reply with a text saying, *"Hey, can't talk* "or *"I'm fine, stop calling me"*. That was nothing like her nor indicative of their relationship. Dani was the first-person Lenox talked to each day, and she made sure to check in with him before she settled in each night. Lenox was a few years older than Daniella, but they were two peas in a pod, which is how Lenox knew something was not right.

It had been almost six months since he had last seen his sister. Their conversation did not go as well as he had hoped. He knew she was pissed at him because he put his foot down as her big brother, but for her to stop talking to him completely was beyond him and unlike her. Though Lenox vowed to never return to Chicago due to getting out of his old lifestyle, he returned anyway, seeking answers about her. No past could keep him from his values: love, loyalty, and family first. The goal was to find answers about Daniella. But after meeting Dahlia, he knew his mission was derailed.

He shifted his focus back to the problem at hand—his sister. He'd questioned so many people he was starting to lose track. Maybe he was responsible for her disappearance. He was no angel, and for that reason couldn't dismiss his actions as one of the reasons Dani was gone. Lenox recalled the night his family died.

Lenox pulled up to the house after getting the hysterical phone call from Dani. There were three police cars, one fire truck, and two ambulances posted on his block. He got out of the car to find his sister, Dani, crying uncontrollably and being consoled by his best friend BG.

"What happened, Bro?" Lenox asked, his eyes darting back and forth between the house, his sister, and the emergency vehicles. BG and Lenox left Dani at the rig while they walked to discuss the possibility of what could have happened.

"Your parents." BG sighed. "Bro, they're gone. I pulled up and saw one of them Latin King symbols in the car that sped off. They gotta be behind this shit, man, because of the missing drugs."

"Nah, folks, I've already spoken to their leader; we're cleared. He knows it wasn't us who hit his spot" Lenox replied.

"Well, maybe one of them lil niggas didn't get the memo, cuz this shit is foul" BG said, consoling his best friend.

Lenox walked over to Dani and held her tightly. He did everything he could to keep the tears from falling from his eyes. He had to be strong for his sister, even though they had both lost their parents. Over the next three months, Lenox dropped at least 15 Latin Kings. He figured one apple spoiled the bunch. Since he didn't know which of them was behind his parents' murders, he wiped out their entire unit.

Lenox believed that Dani going missing and possibly being dead was his karma for killing those Mexican gangbangers two years ago. His guilt was catching up to him. With his parents and sister gone, Lenox had nothing. This is why the intrigue of the girl at the bar was uncanny.

In the twenty-seven years that Lenox had been on this earth, he'd been with plenty of women. He never saw a future with any of them until now. He watched the feisty dark bone the entire time he was at Nobu the other night. He wanted to know her—**had** to know her. But first, he had to take care of some business. He planned to meet with one of his bros' to check on old business. Lenox had been out of the drug and gun game for about 3 years now, but the minute he got back in town, ghosts from the past started to pop up.

***

Naima, Lux, and Keena counted their earnings from the previous night and decided to spend the day splurging on themselves. It was times like this that having a car was necessary, and they were grateful that Lux had her own.

The first stop was the Pretty Kitty Yoni Bar in Merrillville, Indiana. It was run by a chick named Layna. Anytime the girls wanted to steam their vaginas, get some of her homemade soap, or even just a little old-fashioned gossip, Elayna was the girl they called first! The small room draped in pink in black decor was the perfect start to their day. Keena plopped her hips onto the first steam pot that was available, while Naima and Lux spent time perusing through all the herbs and soaps Layna had in stock. After all three girls finished their steam treatment, Lux walked away with two bottles of Blue Klit oil and two oatmeal soap bars, while Naima held on to her bar of Tumeric soap.

Afterward, they decided to stop by Jasmine's Classy Savage pop-up shop, which took place in one of the stores in River Oaks Mall. All three girls picked out the outfit they knew would hug their shapes, turn heads and ultimately get their bag stuffed. Next, they went to get pedicures. Being on their feet all night in 4-inch stilettos took its toll on their foot arches and calves. A hot stone foot massage healed those muscles and provided much-needed relaxation.

The final stop was dinner at El Mariachi, one of the girls' favorite restaurants. The girls ordered a spread of steak tacos on corn tortillas, fresh guacamole, and the spiciest salsa they had. They all waited anxiously until their food arrived. They skimmed through their social media apps and took selfies until the waitress placed the salsa, chips, and margaritas on the table. Lux put a dab of hand sanitizer on each of the girls' hands, then they dug in.

Wiping salsa from her mouth, Naima decided to spark up a conversation. "So, what y'all think about the new girl? I haven't had the chance to spend much time with her.

"She aight. I'll have to kick it with her a little more before I decide how I really feel about her." Lux replied, taking a sip of her margarita.

"Well, I don't like her." Keena said matter-of-factly.

"Why, what happened?" Naima asked curiously, sucking on the lime after downing her tequila shot.

"Keena, that girl ain't did nothing to you." Lux added.

"She came between me and my bag. She ain't willing to get dirty to make some money and ion like that."

"You mad at the girl for not hopping on a random dick? Everybody does not get down like you, Keena."

"And for that reason, the bitch won't be paid like me either. You can talk that shit if you want to, but I know moving forward not to include her on the big bucks.

"Money isn't everything, Keena Beena." Naima said.

"The hell it ain't!" Keena replied, causing all the girls to reflect on their lives before meeting Char.

Naima grew up in a foster home. She never knew her parents and didn't know if she had siblings or not. She and her girlfriend planned on saving money to move to Houston, but their plans took a back seat one night Char approached them at a festival in Washington Park. Charmaine brought both of them on board. Since Naima had the prettier face, she immediately became a Suga Baby, while her girlfriend became one of Charmaine's dancers. Every day Naima wanted to leave, but her girlfriend was addicted to the lifestyle and ignored her requests. That was three years ago. Now they are both knee-deep in the business, and she and her ex barely speak.

Keena's known the streets her whole life. Her mother traded her for a fix and died of an overdose shortly after. The man she sold Keena to had her working the streets at fifteen years old. She had no way to get out until she met Charmaine on her eighteenth birthday. Charmaine knew Keena would be perfect for the pole with her personality and perfect hour-glass shape. After working at the club for two years, she upgraded to being a Suga Baby. Presently, working with Char for seven years, Keena seemed to want something different, but the money pulled her back in every time.

Lux had a different story. She didn't come from poverty. In fact, her family was well off, and for that reason, they tried to control her. They wanted to decide the school she went to, the men she dated, even the clothes she wore. But Lux always had a rebellious spirit. The moment she turned 21, she left her family's mansion in Oakbrook, Illinois, and never looked back. She couldn't even if she wanted to; her family disowned her. One day while working the fragrance section at Macy's, she found herself being approached by Charmaine. Once Charmaine encouraged her to quit, she put her name tag on the counter and walked away. Four years into the game, as Char's most loyal and trusted worker has provided Lux with stacks of cash and the freedom she always wanted.

"She seems very unproblematic. Stays in her room and doesn't say much. I like her." Naima said, snapping the girls from their daydreams and causing Keena to roll her eyes.

Well, ain't nothing wrong with a woman that is sure of herself and has boundaries. Lux added. The girls finished up their food then headed back to the compound.

Chapter Six

Dahlia was adjusting to life without her grandmother better than she had expected. It took some time for her to put things into perspective. Once she realized her grandmother was in a better place and she no longer had to carry her as a burden, she started to feel much better.

Dahlia spent her time either texting Lenox or working for Char. Her social life was trash. She didn't have much of a relationship with Lux, Naima, or Keena. They'd speak to her at events and might make small talk but nothing further. Whenever they went out, Dahlia pretended not to see them. That was her way of not getting her hopes up, expecting them to invite her to go out with them. It was a given they didn't care much for her, and for those reasons, Dahlia was confused when Lux approached her.

"Aye, new girl, come roll with me."

"With you? Nah, I'm good."

"I thought we were cool. What did I miss?" Lux asked curiously.

"We are cordial at best. Lux, you haven't spoken to me in three weeks since that night at Nobu. Now I don't know if I messed up your bag, and you tryna get me back or what?"

"Oh girl, it is what it is. I'm not mad at that at all. You have boundaries; I can do nothing but respect them. I'm just trying to extend an olive branch because I do, in fact, respect how you handled yourself. I know where you stand now, so you and I are good. And you don't have to worry about me putting you in another situation like that. Besides, I don't like sharing my man anyway."

"Who, that old man?" Dahlia asked, laughing.

"Girl, 'the older the berry, the sweeter the juice', or whatever Smokey said." The girls both burst into laughter.

"Where are you going anyway?" Dahlia inquired.

"I'm about to run to the mall in Orland Park."

"I guess I can go. I don't wanna sit in here all day, anyhow. Can you run me to Discovery? It's down the street from the mall." She asked, combing her hair back and putting on a flowered baseball cap.

"Lia, you make enough money here to DISCOVER a better store. Girl, stop wearing those cheap ass clothes and get something out of Nordstrom or Akira at least."

"I wouldn't care if I had ten stacks. I'm still going to get some earrings, sunglasses, and whatever else I see out of Discovery. It's June, all the summer dresses are stocked!! Don't sleep girl, they are the bomb."

The two fast friends headed out of the warehouse to Lux's car. At the very last minute, Keena joined them. She invited herself and refused to take no for an answer. Dahlia didn't mind. On the other hand, Lux preferred to keep her interactions with Keena on a professional level only. "Let's go bitches!" Keena yelled.

The girls cruised in Lux's blue Ford Focus and headed to Orland Mall. When they got there, Dahlia tagged along while Lux and Keena went into the stores that were well out of her budget. They stopped in the Coach store and both walked out with new bags. *Must be nice*, Dahlia thought. After stopping to get some cinnamon pretzel sticks, they ventured into Akira, which was more within Dahlia's price range. The girls tried on different skirts, dresses, and shoes. Dahlia watched as Keena squeezed her hips and thighs into clothes that were too small for her. "Keena, it's a Lane Bryant in here. You can fit the clothes in there for sure," suggested Lux.

"Bitch, how about I fit my fist into your mouth?" Keena laughed.

"I'm just saying, girl, you're stretching all the damn clothes." Dahlia and Lux laughed so hard that Keena got into her feelings.

"Fuck y'all, I don't know why we came to this itty-bitty bitch store anyway."

"Aw girl, come on now, I'm just messing with you." She reassured her.

The trio checked out at the counter, then headed to the food court because, clearly, the pretzel Keena just had wasn't enough. After browsing through their options, they decided to go to Uncle Julio's instead of eating at the mall. The girls engaged in a bit of window shopping then headed to the car. Dahlia opted to not go to Discovery after all since she'd found a few things in Akira and Victoria's Secret.

"I saw that dress, girl. Who are you getting' sexy for?" Keena asked Dahlia.

"This guy I met, he's cool. Ain't nothing serious though we are just talking right now."

"He got a big dick?"

'Keena?!" Lux laughed. "You ain't got no shame!"

"I'm just saying, if it ain't gon make me run, then it ain't gon make me cum! Ya heard me. What's his name? I probably fucked him." Keena laughed although she was dead serious.

"Y'all," Lux said, interrupting their conversation. "Char wants us back at the warehouse now. She said the event is earlier than she anticipated, so we're going to have to skip Uncle Julios." She then turned up WAP and sped down I-80.

They pulled up to the compound, and Keena jumped out of the front seat. "To the money bitches!" She shouted, running toward the front entrance. Lux and Dahlia grabbed the bags out of the trunk and followed behind her.

"Aye, new girl!" Lux said to Dahlia before entering the building. "Keena is cool but keep it professional. Don't tell her shit. She talks too much, and she will tell Char whatever y'all talk about, trust me."

"Got it." Dahlia replied.

Chapter Seven

After talking for about a month or so, Dahlia agreed to go out with Lenox. They spent the majority of their time texting but every so often, he demanded to hear her voice and demanded to know her real name. He was relentless in his efforts pursuing her.

She met him at the carnival, as they previously discussed. The scene brought up many memories of her and her grandmother. Money was scarce growing up, but her granny scraped together whatever cash she had to get them a ticket and at least cotton candy. It didn't bother Dahlia that they couldn't afford to get on the rides. She was just as happy watching the other children enjoy them.

After Lenox got their entry tickets from the booth, he paused and stared at her. Although she kept it simple with a white tank and distressed blue jean shorts, she was strikingly gorgeous. From her chocolate skin to the silver hoops in her ears that complemented her high ponytail, she was beautiful, very barbie doll-like. Lenox proudly took her hand and led them through the crowd of people.

When Lenox found out Dahlia had never actually gotten on carnival rides before, he made sure they rode every single one. From the zipper to the tilt-a-whirl, Dahlia screamed loudly on every ride. After each ride, Lenox made sure to stop and get something to eat. Dahlia noticed two things about Lenox. One, he loved to eat, and two, he must have had a high metabolism. His body was in tip-top shape, even though he went to nearly every booth and gobbled down the trashiest food. She was sure he'd pass out in the July heat from being so full of all the crap he had consumed. Finally, they stopped at this Mexican stand and got the fruity ice cream bar. The couple found an empty table next to the picture booth and sat down to enjoy some casual conversation.

"So, this is your idea of a date?" She teased, hoping he would pick up on her sarcasm.

"Well, I'm sure you could take a break from that fancy nightlife you live, to come slum it with me for a while." He laughed.

"And what makes you think I'm fancy or live a fancy nightlife, as you say?"

"You must have forgotten that I met you with diamonds in your ears and red bottoms on your feet at one of the most expensive hotels in Chicago."

"And? You were at the same hotel with a $30 cigar in your pocket Lenox, but you don't see me making any assumptions about your lifestyle." She responded.

"We ain't talking about me, though; we're talking about you."

She chuckled. "You're funny. I was working. I don't carry myself like that every day."

"How long have you been at your job?" He asked, scooping some of the Mexican corn into his mouth.

"Not long, little over four months."

"Do you like it? Ya know, can you see yourself doing it forever?"

"Forever, not at all. Right now, it's a means to an end. I need both of my feet on the ground so that I won't end up where I was before."

"And where were you before?"

"Is this a job interview? You don't get all my secrets on the first date, Lenox. No matter how charming you may be."

"Finally, you admit the truth. You think I'm charming." He smiled, rubbing his beard. Dahlia couldn't help but notice how smooth his skin looked and how crisp his lining was. She continued to suck on her popsicle.

"You alright" she blushed. Lenox tried to ignore his phone for the tenth time, but after avoiding it for so long, he finally took the call and walked away. After chatting for about five minutes, he headed back to the bench where Dahlia was sitting.

"You mind if we cut this short? I got a run to make." He regrettably asked.

"Are you kicking me to the side to go lay up with somebody else?" She laughed.

"Hell no. As a matter of fact- you can ride with me."

They threw the remaining of their food away, freshened up, and exited the carnival. Dahlia settled in the front seat of Lenox's gray Challenger. He started up the car and immediately cooled them down. She was grateful to be under the air conditioner and out of the heat, which was eerily similar to what the Vegas Heat felt like. Before they pulled off, Lenox feasted his eyes on Dahlia. He noticed her perfectly pedicured feet, milk chocolate scar-free legs, then settled on her breasts. The chill from the air perked her nipples up and Lenox couldn't take his eyes off them.

"Ion know what you looking like that for. You ain't getting nothing over here. You couldn't handle me even if you tried." She teased.

Lenox licked his lips and grinned. He leaned in close enough so they could feel the heat from each other's mouth, but he never kissed her. He studied her eyes, then trailed his fingers from her thighs to the bottom of her shorts. Her breathing became erratic the moment he found her essence. Lenox took his fingers and gently glided them across her yoni lips. He slowly dipped them in her wetness, causing Dahlia to turn away. "Look at *me*," he demanded. Biting her lip, Dahlia's gaze met him again. With intent, Lenox slowly circled her clit, sending Dahlia into a frenzy. Right before she reached her peak, Lenox stopped, creating a puzzled look on her face.

"Now, who can't handle who?" He said, flashing his perfectly white smile. Lenox reached past Dahlia and into his glove compartment. He put on some of the hand sanitizer that was inside of it. He watched as

Dahlia's chest rose and fell as she tried to control her breathing. She didn't move or speak. She was hot, bothered, turned on, and embarrassed.

They drove for about 25 minutes. They could have been at their destination sooner, but Lenox knew Dahlia needed time to gather herself, so he took the long way to the hood. Finally, they stopped on what was labeled one of the deadliest blocks in Chicago.

"Oh, hell no, I'm not getting out of the car." Those were the first words Dahlia said since Lenox toyed with her kitty and emotions.

"Come on, you with me, ain't nobody gon fuck with you. Trust me." He reassured her.

"I'm not worried about that. I can handle myself. It's just-"

"It's a kids' event, Dahlia. Ain't nothing gonna pop off."

That don't mean nothing to these Chicago niggas, she thought. Dahlia got out of the car and held his hand as he guided her through the busy block. King Von "Crazy Story" parts one through three looped on the speakers. When Lenox walked up, the children jumped for joy. He handed them each a five-dollar bill, then led Dahlia to a group of men.

"Fuck took you so long Nigga, you know we do the fireworks every year." One of the guys said, shaking up with Lenox.

"Chill, bro, lemme introduce you to somebody. Dahlia, this is BG- BG Dahlia."

"Ah, so you the one that made my mans forget about the firework show for the kids." He said, extending his hand to her. Dahlia laughed and shook his hand. She sat off to the side and watched Lenox interact with everyone. He was a natural, clearly loved, and his presence commanded respect. The fireworks going off, the kids running around, and looking in the sky with amazement brought warmth to Dahlia's heart. She had been in such a dark space for some time that the smallest things brought her hope and happiness.

Chapter Eight

Another night as a Suga Baby and another chance for the girls to make some coins. Keena, Lux, Naima, and Dahlia found themselves at another one of Charmaine's events, but this time, they had competition. One of Charmaine's clients rented out Three Dots and a Dash for a Bachelor party, and he wanted more attention for his guests than the four girls could handle. Thus, Charmaine brought in six of her dancers to keep everyone entertained.

Since the bar was tiki-themed, the strippers wore coconut bras with thongs and grass skirts. The girls agreed to wear green cocktail dresses with matching leis and hibiscus clips in their hair. Keena, being Keena, decided to "stand out" and wore a cheetah print dress that left nothing to the imagination. When asked why she didn't stick with the theme, she defended her decision by saying the cheetah was the state animal in Hawaii- #LIES.

The minute they touched down, the girls entered the crowd. The Suga Babies pretty much had a free night out because Char's strippers controlled the room, with help from Keena, of course. They provided private dances and who knows what else. See, the rules didn't apply to all of Char's workers. While the Suga Babies weren't allowed to date or sleep with the clientele, the strippers had no rules. They could fuck for free if they wanted to, and Charmaine wouldn't bat an eye.

Dahlia flirted here and there, rubbed a shoulder or two, but those men craved something different, and we all know Dahlia wasn't going. She saw Naima chatting in the corner, so she joined Lux at the bar. They both sipped on two frozen painkillers and complained about this night being a waste of their time. Lux talked about missing out on time with Black, while Dahlia whined about missing Lenox.

"You really like him, huh?" Lux asked. "Yall been talking for a while now".

"Yes, I do. But this no dating policy is stopping me from taking it further."

"Lia, girl, do what the fuck you want to do. Just keep it to yourself. What Char doesn't know won't hurt her. And you definitely ain't gotta worry about me saying nothing. We all got our secrets." She said, toasting Lia.

"I heard that," Lia replied. She ordered another frozen painkiller when an unexpected guest leaned on the bar against her.

"Thought you looked familiar. I watched you from across the room all night. Now, what would my mans say if he could see you or if I told him what I saw?"

"I'm hoping we can keep this between us." Dahlia replied, looking BG in his eyes.

"You don't know me like that shawty. My loyalty is to Smoke, not you. You ain't got no business asking me to keep a secret for you."

"Smoke?" She asked, confused. BG chuckled.

"You obviously don't know "Lenox" either if you didn't know the streets know him as Smoke. That's what happens when you mess around with people you barely know, people that's out of your league."

"If you watched me across the room 'all night' like you claimed to have, then you know there is nothing to tell. What I'm doing is flirting. It's no different than a guy zooming in on a pretty face and ass that walks past him."

"It's a lot different, cuz you're getting paid for this shit, lil mama." BG said, taking another shot to the head.

"The name is Dahlia. Listen, tell Lenox or don't tell him, I truly don't care. We aren't exclusive, and furthermore, I'm a grown-ass woman. I don't need to explain shit to you or nobody else."

"Calm down, shorty. If you're going to be doing this kind of work, you'll need somebody to protect you. Take my number. You call me anytime you get into trouble." Dahlia hesitantly took out her phone and added BG's number to it. "You ain't gotta worry about me sayin shit to Smoke."

"I was never worried." She said, walking away. Dahlia was headed to the table where she saw Lux, Naima, Keena, and one of the strippers. Dahlia came in at the end of the conversation, but just in time for the bullshit.

"If you gon wear animal print, at least weigh less than the animal HOE!" The stripper spat at Keena. Before anyone knew what was happening, Keena picked up one of the drink mugs and slammed it into the stripper's face. Dahlia was knocked to the floor by another stripper, who ran to jump in. Lux and Naima started swinging, as did Dahlia when she got back to her feet. The guys were cheering as if they were watching a wet t-shirt contest. The security managed to break up the brawl and tossed everyone out of the bar. The Suga Babies headed to the SUV they originally arrived in while the strippers jumped in the van behind it. Char got into the SUV slamming the door after her.

"Y'all bitches really out here fighting? That's a $1,000 fine, Keena!" Charmaine yelled, causing Keena to nearly choke.

"WHAT?! FOR WHAT CHAR, THE BITCH STARTED WITH ME."

"First of all, lower your muthafuckin voice when you address me! You're supposed to be smart enough to not engage. She knew what to say to push your buttons, and you took the bait! You know them girls wanna be in your position, the fuck is you entertaining them for?"

"But"-

"Ain't no but, Keena. You make me question promoting you every day. You wanna be in the gutter? Fine. You can start working the poles again. And you're suspended from the next event." As Charmaine spoke, Keena decided to soften her tone because her pockets were getting hit in every direction.

"Char, you're making me pay a $1,000 fine and suspending me from the next event? That's some bullshit."

"If you ask me, I should fire you. I saw you go in the back with one of the guests. So let me be clear to all of y'all one last time. Do not sleep with the clients or their guests. I'm not a Madam, and this ain't a muthafuckin brothel! If I find out it's some shady shit going on, I'm shutting this down. Y'all hear what I'm saying?" She asked, looking at the girls.

They all nodded. Naima and Dahlia had nothing to worry about for the most part. Lux and Keena, on the other hand, made it a habit to get more money by giving up the goodies. Dahlia wasn't necessarily in the clear, though. Because like Lux said a couple hours earlier, they all had their secrets.

Between the standoff with BG and the fight Keena had, Dahlia was exhausted. The minute they got back to the warehouse, she took a bath and fell asleep on the phone with Lenox.

Chapter Nine

Dahlia managed to spend every free moment available to her with Lenox. She was dedicated to getting her clients out of the way as quickly as possible just to be with him. They spent most of their time together from Sundays to Thursdays because the likelihood of Char having an event during those days was slim to none. Dahlia would leave the warehouse first thing in the morning and wouldn't return until late at night. Dahlia and Lenox spent lots of their time at community service events, cruising in his car, or chilling at the lakefront. For the first time in the few months, they'd been spending time together, they decided to stay in and have dinner at his crib. Lenox opened the door to his studio and looked Dahlia up and down.

"I thought you wanted to stay in tonight? You look good." Lenox added, placing a kiss on her forehead.

"Thanks," she smiled. "It's just a sundress, we are staying in. What movies do they have on Prime?" She asked, walking over to the kitchen sink to wash her hands. She sat her wristlet on the counter and dried them, before joining him on his couch.

"Shid, a bunch of nothing." He replied, continuing to scroll through the collection of movies.

"That's because you're only looking for old gangsta movies. I'll find something." She said after she took the remote from him. Lenox washed his hands then opened the Thai food she brought over. Before digging in, he took a beer out of the fridge for himself and a bottle of water for her. They settled on some random made-for-tv movie and dug into their food. Their meal was over before they knew it, leaving both of them wanting more. Two hours later and thirty minutes into the next movie, they were both hungry again.

"See, that's why I don't like eating out," Dahlia complained.

"What you talm bout?"

"Folks spend all that money on small portions and don't be satisfied. Next time, I'll just grab some groceries and cook. All you do is eat restaurant food." She teased.

"Man, you can't cook."

"Boy, you crazy! I was in culinary school before everything happened with my grandmother. I know my way around the kitchen. Only thing I'm worried about is the food industry being so massive. I will have tons of hurdles to jump just to get into the top kitchens. There's way too much competition out there." I do not want to always feel like I am struggling to get to the top.

"Let me show you something real quick," he said. Lenox led Dahlia to the mirror by the entrance of the studio. They both faced toward the mirror. He caressed her cheek and lifted her chin. "You see her, right there? She is your ONLY competition and nobody else."

Dahlia melted into his arms, then met him with hesitation when he kissed her neck. "I gotta go, there's so-" Dahlia's sentence was brought to a halt once Lenox passionately pressed his lips against hers. Their tongues playfully massaged each other. Dahlia avoided Lenox's gaze and touch throughout the majority of their time together. Thus, her resistance to his persistence intensified her sex appeal. He had to have her.

"Don't run now." He breathed into her ear. Dahlia's yoni throbbed with excitement and leaked with anticipation. With her back pressed against the brick wall, Lenox fell to his knees with the hopes of getting a taste of her juices. But Dahlia had craved Lenox long enough and needed him inside of her expeditiously.

"Take me to your bed." She begged. Lenox carried her to his bed. He pulled her dress over her head and her body shuddered while he trailed kisses from her thighs to her belly button, then her breasts. His tongue circled her nipples, causing her to tremble. He gently bit her lip and she sucked on his. He teased her opening with the head of his dick before gliding into her wet tunnel.. She was taken by surprise and dug into his back when he entered her essence. "Wait, Lenox." She pleaded. Lenox paused, giving Dahlia time to adjust to his size. She let out a low whimper as he eased the majority of his pole inside of her. Her body surrendered as each stroke put her into a state of bliss. Lenox dug deep into her. Dahlia gripped him tightly as she pulsated on his member, trying to stifle the moan that eventually managed to escape from her mouth. Lenox groaned and nibbled on her ear, before flipping her onto her stomach. She eagerly arched her back and awaited his next move. Smacking her on her cheeks, he plunged into her again. Dahlia gripped the sheets and buried her head into the pillow. She screamed in pleasure while Lenox enjoyed the view of watching her further lose control. Lenox lightly pulled her hair, bringing her up from the pillow.

"You like this shit?" He asked, smacking her ass.

Dahlia's words were stuck at the back of her throat. She moaned, throwing her ass back while Lenox continued to maneuver in and out of her. "Answer me." He demanded, smacking her chocolate cheeks again, this time with more force.

"Y-ye-yes!" Dahlia cried out. Lenox applied more pressure, continuing to ravage her insides. After a few more strokes, Lenox released himself. Dahlia lay there, trying to gain her composure. Her labored breathing made it difficult for her body to recover from a sensation she had never felt before. In that very moment, Dahlia was fucked, literally and figuratively. Because she had deliberately broken the most important rule- do not fall in love.

The following morning while Lenox was still sleeping, she recalled their conversation and him believing she could not prepare a meal. Driven to prove him wrong, Dahlia managed to sneak away to get groceries to make him breakfast. There was an Asian market down the street from his condo. She stopped there and picked up a fresh cut of salmon and two large grapefruit, amongst other items. Lenox helped Dahlia realize that she could still pursue her dreams, and it was never too late. He also laid her completely out the previous night, and she had no choice but to K.O. The least she could do was fix the man a meal.

When Dahlia got back to the condo, she climbed back into his white tank that she slept in and immediately got to work. She worked quietly and efficiently, hoping to not wake him. She smiled while cracking the eggs and putting the final touches on their meal. He awoke to the smell of the food and didn't hesitate to dig in.

"What's all this?" He asked, kissing her forehead. They indulged in her layout and continued to talk.

"It's smoked salmon eggs benedict. Hope you're not allergic to capers. Then, if all else fails and you don't like my food, I blended you a boring-ass banana and strawberry smoothie. What kills me is you eat all this restaurant food, but think these lil smoothies can combat all the other crap you put in your system."

Lenox was damn near licking the plate by the time Dahlia had finished presenting the dish to him.

"Damn, I ain't had a breakfast this good since..."

"Since what?"

"Well, it's been a while. My mother used to make pancakes, and she would make a separate batter just for me. My sister was allergic to cinnamon, but I loved it. So, she would make two batters, then at the end sprinkle more cinnamon on top and say *keep this between you and mommy*." Lenox smiled as he recalled his precious memory. . Dahlia smiled, listening to him and was happy he seemed to be opening up.

"You don't talk about your family much."

"Naw, I don't." He said, sipping the freshly squeezed grapefruit juice that was placed before him. Dahlia waited for him to offer more insight into his family, but when he didn't, she changed the subject.

"So, how was it?" Dahlia asked.

"Ummm, it was okay- just okay." He replied.

"What?" She yelled, tossing a strawberry at him.

"Nah, I'm bullshitting. The shit was fye!" He nodded.

"See, I had to show you better than I could tell you."

"At least you keep your word about something!" He said, taunting the feisty chocolate barbie.

"What do you mean?"

He walked over to Dahlia, towering over her as he stood behind her. He rubbed her shoulders and kissed her neck. "If I can recall, on our first date, you told me I couldn't handle you. I proved you wrong that night and multiple times last night." He flirted.

Dahlia's face flushed. She thought about how her mouth always gets her in trouble. And though last night was nothing short of amazing, she couldn't believe how much of a beast he was in bed. Her knees buckled just thinking about it.

"Well, I may not be a match for you in the sheets, but ya girl can cook."

"So, you my girl?" He asked, finishing off his glass of grapefruit juice.

"Wait, I didn't mean it like that." She blushed.

"You meant it...I do, too." He smiled. They headed to his bed for a morning lovemaking session before she headed back to the warehouse later.

***

"Damn girl, you got me weak." BG said, smacking Keena on her ass as she slid out the bed.

"You ready for round 4" Keena smiled, leaning over and reaching through the slit of his boxers.

"Shorty, I ain't got no energy left, and I think you broke my dick. I couldn't get hard even if I wanted to. Grab my stash out the freezer for me." He said. Keena got up and went to the kitchen. She switched her hips as her thighs crashed into each other. Keena was cool, but what BG loved most about her was her body. He worshipped every inch of it each moment he had a chance. They'd been kicking it for a minute now. Keena hoped he was her ticket to exiting her current lifestyle, but he had no intentions of getting serious with her. After preparing the blunt, Keena flamed it up. She took three pulls then passed it to BG.

"Baby, when are we gonna go on a real date?"

"We have been on real dates," he said, blowing the smoke out of his mouth.

"Going to the lake in the dark alone is not a date. I wanna be around people, so they will know I'm your girl."

"You mean to tell me the lakefront is not a real date? I thought bitches liked that kind of shit. I was being romantic."

"Nah, bruh, it's a sneaky link, and I think you know that. You ain't trying to be seen with me in public, probably cuz you got other Hoes."

"Aye, which Ho am I with now? What I do when you ain't around don't have shit to do with you. We having fun, don't fuck up a good thing."

"It's been 5 months, though." She whined.

"Look, you my bitch. If that ain't good enough for you, then get the fuck on. I don't need complaining ass Hoes around me. Matter of fact, get the fuck out." BG was easy to anger, especially when people asked too many questions or pointed out his faults. It made him feel less than, and he was a real nigga, so you couldn't tell him shit.

"Wait, baby, I'm sorry. I know my role."

"Then act like it." BG said, getting out of the bed and heading to the shower.

Keena watched from a distance hoping not to piss him off further. BG was everything to her. He was a little rough around the edges, but he was the only man that could keep up with her sexually. Keena didn't know much about his life outside of the time they spent together. But one thing was for sure, He was a smart-street nigga. She knew he had money; that was clear looking at his house and cars. But still, there was something about him that kept her intrigued. "Where are you going?" She asked hesitantly once he exited the shower.

"Going to meet one of my guys, so get dressed. You can walk out with me." Keena slid on some leggings and a crop top shirt. "Aye, I've been meaning to ask you, don't y'all got a new girl at yo job?"

"Yeah, Lia, she's cool. She keeps her head down. Why do you ask me that?"

"I know somebody that may know her, just making sure she is legit."

"Oh, well yeah, Lia cool. She doesn't cross the line with the clients, and she definitely ain't letting them cross the line with her."

"Word?"

"Yep, she's solid. Is she one of your friends' girls or something? Ohh, we should go on a double date. What's his name? I'mma text her now."

"Bitch is you crazy?" BG asked, smacking the phone out of her hand and grabbing her chin. "This should go without saying, keep yo fuckin mouth closed. Don't you eva let my name come out your mouth to NOBODY, you hear me?" Keena nodded. BG kissed her on her lips. "Just keep an eye on her. Any move she makes, I want to know about it." He grabbed his wallet and the keys to his Mercedes C63S and walked out with Keena trailing behind.

Chapter Ten

BG and Lenox rode down Lakeshore Drive blasting the latest Future song. BG turned the radio down and made a bold statement, catching Lenox off guard.

"Aye, man, leave that bitch alone."

"Who?" Lenox asked, genuinely confused.

"That Dahlia bitch"

"Bro don't disrespect my woman. You don't even know her."

"Actually, I do know her, well I know of her. And if I tell you what type of shit, she into, you ain't gon fuck with her no more." Lenox peered at BG, and after more than enough silence, he urged him to share the information he had on Dahlia.

"What nigga? How do you know her?" Lenox asked.

"Mannnnnnn, shorty a hoe."

"Get the fuck outta here. That's what you came up with?" Lenox laughed

"Nah, for real, bruh. She works at a hoe house, no lie. Them bitches be going on dates with rich niggas, fucking em too, and getting paid."

"How do you know all of this?"

"Because I was fuckin a couple of them for a while. That shit dead now, though." He said, taking a puff of his blunt.

Lenox was silent. He and BG had been friends since they were in high school. He had no reason to lie to him about anything, but at the same time, neither did Dahlia. He planned on getting to the bottom of BG's claims. Since it had been a week since the last time he had seen his lady, he immediately texted Dahlia so they could get together.

***

As always, Lenox picked Dahlia up from a random location instead of her home, something he had not noticed previously. Before arriving at Lenox's place, they stopped at a farmers' market up north to pick up some fresh veggies so Dahlia could make them dinner. While they were at the market, Dahlia picked up a tomato, examined it closely, and even smelled it before she purchased it. Dahlia raved about the importance of fresh produce as a chef, but Lenox paid little attention. He trailed behind her in silence while he continued to try to wrap his mind around the information BG gave him. He watched Dahlia pick out a bushel of romaine lettuce, a cucumber, two potatoes, some cheese, and a fresh cut of ribeye, then they headed to his condo.

When they got to Lenox's place, Dahlia found herself being the only one trying to converse while Lenox sat in silence. He complimented her on how juicy her steak was but didn't offer much more conversation.

Dahlia searched through the new releases on prime until Lenox's deep voice broke the awkward silence.

"Aye, why you don't be letting me pick you up from your crib?" Lenox asked.

"Because I have several roommates and the person in charge does not like random people over." She explained, continuing to peruse through the movie catalog, seemingly unbothered by the question or her response.

"Yeah, but I ain't random, yo. I'm your man. Have been for a while."

"True, but when you are renting a place instead of owning one, you gotta follow other people's rules." She shrugged.

"And you said you was in customer service, retail, or whatever, right?"

"I said I was an image consultant, and what's with the third degree?" It seemed as if Dahlia had a response for everything Lenox asked her. That only upset him more because he felt like her answers were contrived. Before he knew it, Lenox lost his cool.

"Look, is you out there fucking other niggas? Cuz I ain't sign up to be with a liar and definitely didn't sign up to be with a ho!"

Dahlia was taken aback by the words that had come from his lips, and before she knew it, she slapped Lenox so loud that the sound echoed off the walls. Without saying a word, she threw the throw pillow at him, then cleared the dishes they ate out of and sat them on the countertops. Finally, she slid her shoes on and started collecting her things from his coffee table. She headed to the front door, then stopped to address his disrespect.

"Let me tell you something. You asked me very simple questions, and I answered them the way I saw fit. I did not lie to you about anything. I am not ashamed of shit because I haven't done anything, nor do I have anything to hide. I go on dates with men, and I get paid for it. Do you know where I was before I started this hustle? NO! You don't. I was sleeping in my fucking car. A car with no heat or air conditioning, living off chips and candy. Taking showers in the nursing home my grandmother was in. You really think I'mma apologize for lucking up on something like this? I sleep very well at night because I can look at myself in the mirror knowing what my limits are and that I'm not degrading myself. If that's too much for you to handle, say that! You pursued me! Not the other way around."

"Yo, don't act like a nigga just supposed to be okay with this shit. Especially when you wasn't one hundred from the start."

"Lenox, where do you work? How's YOUR family? Do you have a dog, a cat, cousins, parents? Oh, that's right, I forgot. We don't talk about you! At least I'm honest, ain't no telling what skeletons you got in your closet."

"You know what, Dahlia? I'mma fall back for a while."

"Right, that's what I thought. You wanna avoid your shit."

"I came back to Chicago to take care of some business and I can see I'm getting off track. I don't need to get into anything serious. Let me take you home."

"Wow! Really Lenox? Naw, I'm good; I don't need a ride. You know hoes get around." She spat before storming out.

Dahlia stood in front of his building, waiting on her Uber to show up. When she got into the car, she looked up and saw Lenox standing in the window. *He had some fuckin nerve. I knew this shit would happen.* Dahlia reminded herself as she rode back to the compound.

Chapter Eleven

Dahlia was disappointed but frustrated, more than anything, at the situation between her and Lenox. She had no choice but to keep it moving. Because at the end of the day, she was all she had. Although she walked out on Lenox nearly two weeks ago, they kept the communication going. He insisted on seeing her multiple times, but Dahlia had to teach him a lesson. She refused each of his attempts, which only pissed Lenox off further.

One of Dahlia's loyal customers booked her for a company dinner, as he always did. She pretended to be his girlfriend and arm candy. In return, he made sure to keep their interactions strictly professional. Dahlia never had to worry about him trying anything with her, and for that, she was grateful. She met him at Ruth's Chris steakhouse downtown.

At the table sat Dahlia, her client, and two other couples. The best thing about clients like him was, not only did Dahlia get paid, but she got a free meal, too. She made sure to order different items, then she'd try to replicate the dishes at a later date to keep her culinary skills sharp. Dahlia made small talk with the women at the table until she was interrupted by a tap on her shoulder.

"Scuse me, I need to talk to you for a minute." Though the voice was familiar, Dahlia was still shocked when she turned around and saw Lenox standing beside her. Dahlia had to think quickly on her feet because her money was in jeopardy.

"Excuse me, honey." She said to her client, placing the napkin that was on her lap onto white cloth that covered the table. Mr. Phillips, and everyone at the table fixed their eyes on Lenox, who grabbed her arm and escorted her away from them. She smiled and eased out of his grip, so she would not alarm her client or his coworkers. They stood in the private hallway that housed the coat check closet.

"I've been calling you all day. What are you doing here?" He snapped.

"Would you lower your voice?" She urged, pulling him into the coat closet and locking the door. "I am working, Lenox. I told you I was going to be busy this weekend." She whispered.

"You call this shit work? If you wanna fuck other people, just say that."

"That's your last time calling me a ho. What part of this don't you understand? I haven't messed around with anybody but you. But if I wanted to suck and fuck every dick up in this muthafucka, that's my business. Don't turn into a jealous boyfriend, now! I'm not your woman!"

"Aye, man, stop playing with me."

"Lenox, you made it crystal clear you were not looking for anything serious. I am working the same job I was working when you met me. And it's still the same damn job that made you say you ain't looking for anything to hold you back; nothing has changed."

"I don't want you doing this shit no more, ion want my girl out here-"

"Again, I'm not your girl. You made that-" Before she could finish her statement, Lenox grabbed her face and stuck his tongue in her mouth. She leaned into the counter and allowed him to prop her leg up. He fell to his knees, gently caressing her kitty, then slid her black lace panties to the side. Her knees immediately buckled at the touch of his tongue separating her flower petals and gliding across her bud. "Shit," she moaned.

"You my woman." He breathed into her. She threw her head back in total bliss. "Tell me you my woman." He continued while sliding his fingers inside of her, assaulting her yoni with his tongue.

"Yea." She moaned.

"Say that shit!" He demanded.

"...I'm.... your woman." She breathed heavily. Lenox held her in place, his fingers stroking her walls as she reached her climax. Lenox traced kisses up her thighs until finally landing on her lips.

"You gon have to let that gig go, baby. Nothing about it is legit, and it most likely won't end well. You feel me?"

Dahlia's heart danced around her chest as she tried to come down from the high Lenox had her feeling.

He had a way with his mouth, no pun intended, and she knew he was right. "I got you." She finally replied. Lenox slapped her on her ass before she left the coat closet. When Dahlia got back to the table with Mr. Phillips and his colleagues, he asked if everything was ok. She smiled and joined in on their meaningless discussion. Dahlia peered at Lenox who was standing at the bar. He smirked, caressed his beard, threw a shot back, and left.

***

Later that week, Charmaine scheduled a meeting with Dahlia. Dahlia didn't know what it was about because she had not had any run-ins with any of the other workers or her clients. When she sat down, Charmaine avoided the small talk and got right down to business.

"Mr. Phillips told me some gentleman interrupted your evening with him. Who was it?"

"It was an old friend," she replied. Charmaine stared at Dahlia. She offered her time to be honest, but she jumped headfirst into the lie, which only pissed Charmaine off.

"Lia, I hold you to a different standard because I see a lot of myself in you, and I really thought I could trust you not to screw up my money. But it seems like you're breaking rules. I told you no relationships; I was clear on that." Charmaine said.

Dahlia contemplated her response. While she was grateful for the opportunity Charmaine presented her with, she knew she couldn't jump back into culinary arts,hold on to Lenox, the job, and her dignity. While she was happy to have some sort of financial stability, she was happier with Lenox.

"I need to know if this is something you truly want to do. I'm not going to waste my time investing into you if--"

"Investing in me, what do you mean?" Dahlia asked,

"Let me show you something. Follow me." Dahlia followed Charmaine through a secret door behind a plant in her office that led them to level two. They walked into a small room that had three tables set up and two girls at each of them. They were stuffing what looked like candy into makeup holders and shampoo bottles. All of the girls were topless, with thongs on. "This is another one of my operations. I make party pills; they're called Pink Ladies. I distribute them in Mexico. See Dahlia, you catch on fast and you're discreet. I would like for you to be my point person for Mexico." Dahlia looked around with wide-eyed wonder.

"Wow...Char...this sounds incredible. "But"- she paused. "I'm sorry, I'll have to pass. I got goals. I have a career in mind. I can't uproot my life to be a Queen Pin in Mexico."

"You're so cute," she replied, laughing hysterically at Dahlia. "You would be more like a courier. You're required to make one drop once a month. You keep the entire cut from your deliveries. You're not actually traveling to Mexico, you're just the point person for that country. Anything comes up missing, it's on you. Oh, and Lia, I wasn't asking. You'll be a Suga Baby and

Pink Ladie. And to be clear suga, the only 'QUEEN' around here is me." She said, walking away.

No matter what Dahlia did, she seemed to be sinking deeper into Charmaine's world. One minute she's an entertainer, the next minute, she's playing as if she's Tommy Vercetti. She was getting further away from her dreams of being a chef. It felt like she was losing her grip on life, and she didn't know how to fix it. Furthermore, she had no way to explain this to Lenox.

Chapter Twelve

Lux was over the moon because she knew that within a couple of hours, she'd be rolling in the sheets with her boo. More importantly, she knew that after tonight, she would no longer be an employee of Charmaine's. She planned to tell Charmaine she wanted to get out of the business, especially since her three-year contract expired at the end of the month. Knowing Charmaine, she'd make her work every day until the contract expired, which was only in four days. Lux didn't know how much time she'd be able to spend with Dahlia once she moved out of the warehouse, so she invited her out for a drink. Of course, they decided to get a drink at Nobu because that's where Lux would be meeting Black soon. The bartender placed two martinis in front of the girls. They sipped as they engaged in conversation.

"Lux, I need to talk to you about something."

"What's up?" Lux asked, concerned.

"Char offered me another job." Dahlia said with a half-smile on her face.

"Nope. Don't do it." Lux replied. She took the olive from the Martini glass and popped it in her mouth.

"You don't even know what it is." She laughed.

"Yes, I do, love. She wants you to be a point person for Pink Ladies, right?"

"Dang, how did you know?"

"Because she asked me, and I told her no."

"So, I'm her sloppy seconds, is what you're telling me?" She laughed.

"Naw, you're the one to watch, to be honest. Char don't just let anybody in her business. She sought you to be a Suga Baby, I'm sure. She sees something in you and believes she can trust you. That can work in your favor...or it could work against you." Lux replied.

"Then why are you telling me not to get involved? I need the money."

"Because all money ain't good money, sis. Don't get in too deep. And in terms of time, it's just another debt you'll owe to Charmaine."

"Char doesn't really take no for an answer." Dahlia said, sinking into her chair.

"Well, you better figure something out, Teresa Mendoza, because if you start saying yes now, you won't be able to tell her no later. And what would your man say about that?" Lux winked. The girls finished their drinks. With Charmaine out of town and a free weekend ahead of her, Dahlia couldn't wait until Lenox picked her up so she could spend her time worry-free in his arms.

***

Dahlia realized she'd left her phone at the bar. She was so anxious to see Lenox that she ran to him and left the poor galaxy on the bar when he said he was outside. She called the bar to see if they had it there, but they denied it. She didn't know Lux's number by heart, so she called the hotel back to be transferred to Black's room. After several attempts, Dahlia decided to drop by after leaving Lenox's place the next day. And although she dreaded the idea of seeing Mr. Greystone again, she knew going up to his room was the only way she'd get her things.

Dahlia got off the elevator and headed to his suite. When she approached the door, she noticed it was partially open. She entered the room and immediately got an eerie feeling. The bed was undone, a lamp was knocked over, and little pills were on the carpet. Dahlia followed the trail of pills to the bathroom and screamed in horror at the sight before her. Mr. Greystone - with a towel wrapped around his waist; sat against the shower door with a bullet to his head. Dahlia put her hand over her mouth to stop herself from gagging. She backed up into the closet and fell after she tripped over something. On the floor, she came face-to-face with her friend. "Lux." She whimpered. Dahlia ran to the hotel phone and called the paramedics.

Chapter Thirteen

Dahlia and Lenox went out to breakfast two days after Lux and Mr. Greystone were found dead at the hotel. She was sad that her new friend was gone, heartbroken even. More importantly, she was confused about who would want to hurt them. *Why did I have to be the one to find them of all people,* she thought.

"Baby, you're not gonna eat anything?" He asked, slicing into her stuffed French toast for her. "I need you to eat because what I am about to tell you- will catch you off guard."

"What is it, Lenox? I don't think I can take much more."

"I need you to listen to me. In about ten minutes, FBI agents are going to storm in here and arrest you for the murder of Black and Lux. They'll also arrest you for conspiracy to cover up the disappearance of Daniella LeBlanc."

"What do you mean? I didn't have shit to do with what happened to Lux. She was dead when I got there! I told you that, I told *them* that! How do you even know Lux...or Black. She asked, confused. "And who is Daniella?" She exclaimed.

"I swear I ain't mean to hurt you. I just needed answers about my sister's case. I didn't know I would meet you. I didn't know I would uncover money laundering, drugs, none of this shit."

"Uncover? Lenox, what are you talking about?"

"I am a detective. I have been working with the FBI undercover for about six months, looking for my sister, Daniella. She used to work for Charmaine until she disappeared." Dahlia looked at Lenox in utter disbelief. He lied, lied by omission. Made her fall for him, made her love him and it was all a *lie*.

"You're a fuckin fraud, Lenox! So everything was a hoax? Bumping into me at the bar, the dates, everything! I let my guard down, and you used me!"

"I didn't plan this, Dahlia. I was undercover watching the other girls. I did not know who you were or that you were part of them, honestly. I never lied about how I felt about you. I care for you."

"Fuck out of here. You don't care for me or about me because, if you did, my life would not be on the line. Why the hell am I being arrested? I am not the head bitch in charge. I don't have anything to do with any of this. I was with you! You know that! You know *me*, Lenox."

"I know it's Charmaine who runs the show. You just need to say it. Don't be stupid, Dahlia. Going down for this shit, trying to be loyal to somebody that ain't being loyal to you. FBI knows you met with Black on two different occasions; the first night we met and the last night he was alive. As private as Black

Greystone is, ask yourself how they knew of you guys' interaction. Something ain't right."

"Charmaine is out of town, Lenox. She hasn't said anything. She doesn't even know what's happening."

"That's a smart woman. She has eyes and ears everywhere; you're crazy if you don't believe it."

Just then, two FBI agents walked up to the front door. Lenox held his head down as a look of sadness and disappointment fell across his face. He took the cuffs from his back pocket and stood up.

"Dahlia Greene, you're under arrest for tampering with evidence, conspiracy to cover up a crime, and the murder of Luxine Maxwell and Black Greystone. You have the right to remain silent. Anything you say can and will be used against you in the court of law. You have the right to an attorney. If you cannot afford an attorney, one will be appointed to you."

When he stood behind Dahlia to cuff her, his familiar scent of cologne and coconut oil filled her nostrils. At one point, his scent brought Dahlia to her knees, but now it only brought tears to her eyes. She was terrified. Dahlia felt alone and betrayed.

Lenox led her outside of the diner where the two FBI agents stood with another undercover officer. The plainclothes officer opened the door while Lenox escorted her to it.

"Trust me, baby, I got you." He said before closing her into the car.

The drive to the precinct was short. Dahlia was in a daze. She felt sick to her stomach and her vision was blurry. She was sure her blood pressure had skyrocketed. It was evident her anxiety was getting the best of her. She came up with several scenarios of her dying as an old woman in prison, being jumped by a stud named Barbara, or getting stabbed in her side in the shower and bleeding to death under the cold shower water. Now sure, all the movies she watched over the years contributed to those thoughts. But the truth was, those movies could very well be her reality since she had those charges hanging over her head.

***

Dahlia fiddled her thumbs as she replayed the previous night's events in her mind over and over. She felt like she was in an everlasting nightmare and prayed to wake up soon. The metal chair she sat in at the interrogation room squeaked no matter how slight her movements were. She was cold, uncomfortable, exhausted, and ready to get the interrogation over with.

"Ms. Greene, my name is Agent Walker, this is Agent Knox, and you already know Detective Leblanc." He said as he motioned to Lenox. "Where were you the night of the murder of Luxine and Black Greystone?"

"I was with my boyf- Detective LeBlanc." She stated.

"All night?"

Dahlia cleared her throat. "Yes, all night."

"Were you at Nobu Hotel at any time earlier than that?"

"Yes, earlier that evening. I went to have a drink at the bar in the lobby with Lux, then Detective LeBlanc picked me up."

"Did Luxine mention the plans she had for the rest of the night?" The agent asked.

"She just said she had a date. She didn't say with whom, the time, or where the date was going to take place." Dahlia said

"If you didn't know who she had a date with, how did you know to head to Mr. Greystone's suite to get what was it? Your phone from her, correct?"

"Because her date and where she settled for the remainder of the night could have been with two different people in her line of work."

"Ah, so you're saying she could have entertained a client, then retired for the evening with Mr. Greystone?"

"Yes."

"And why didn't you call her before you headed back to the hotel to get your phone?" Dahlia sighed.

"Because I don't know her number off the top of my head."

"Where did you and Detective LeBlanc go?"

"Sir, I don't see how that's relevant to my friend's death.." Dahlia replied.

"It's not relevant." Lenox interrupted. "She answered the questions; she's done here. I need the room. Turn the camera off."

"What? Man, hell nah. She's a witness, the camera stays on." Agent Walker demanded.

"Turn the fuckin camera off!" Lenox bellowed, knocking the camera off of the tripod. You and I both know she had nothing to do with this. Her being picked up has served its purpose".

"You're out of line and on thin ice, Detective. Don't forget we know where your bodies are buried as well." Agent Walker threatened as he responded to Lenox's outrage. After the two agents left the room, Lenox sat in the chair opposite of Dahlia.

"Listen, I love you. I never felt this way about a woman before. There is nothing I wouldn't do to protect the people I love. I had to bring you in here. It was the only way to make sure that Charmaine wouldn't single you out. You were the last one physically seen with Lux. It would have been odd if you weren't questioned."

"How do you know her? What the hell is going on?"

"My sister worked for her. For a while, I ain't know what the fuck she was doin', or into until I had a couple of people start watching her. When I found out what she was into, I told her to stop, or I would come shut all that shit down. After that, she stopped answering the phone and wouldn't text me back. The people I had watching her said they stopped seeing her out with the other girls. So, I came here, waited and watched, and I've been investigating her ever since."

"So now what, Lenox?"

"We move on. I can use you Dahlia. All you gotta do is cooperate. The closer you get to Charmaine, the quicker I can get answers about my sister. She is still in this world. I can feel her."

"One minute you're asking me to quit, the next minute you want me to play inspector gadget for you. You want me to stick around now because it suits you, right?"

"I wanted you to get out before you got in too deep. Don't think for one second that the trail to my sister turns cold if you decide to quit working for Charmaine. If anything, it will be easier with you close by. But either way, I will find out what happened to her".

Dahlia looked around at the stale walls, then back into Lenox's eyes. Everything had been a blur, but truthfully, Lenox had nothing to lie to her about. Still, if Charmaine was as conniving as he'd made her seem, then maybe she shouldn't be working for her. A thunderstorm of thoughts flooded Dahlia's brain. Lenox searched her eyes, hoping she would accept his apology, accept *him,* and that they could move forward.

"Are we good?" Lenox asked, interrupting her thoughts.

"I don't know. I need time to wrap my head around this." She replied. Dahlia rushed back to the warehouse after receiving a text from Charmaine. She was sure that Charmaine was back and was aware that Lux was gone, so she didn't look forward to facing Charmaine or the reality of her life.

***

Dahlia walked into Charmaine's office. For the first time since Dahlia met her, she looked frazzled. She was smoking a cigarette and leaning back in her chair. Naima stood against the wall with her head down while Keena sat in the chair crying uncontrollably.

"And where the hell have you been?" She asked as Dahlia closed the door behind her. At first, Dahlia planned to lie, but she thought about Lenox stating Charmaine has eyes and ears everywhere and knew the lie could backfire on her.

"Jail."

"Jail? What the fuck did y'all get yourselves into? Somebody better start talking." Charmaine looked around as the three grown women turned into five year olds, not knowing how to control their emotions and keeping their mouths closed like they were afraid to talk.

"SPEAK!" She yelled. Naima spoke up as loud as she could over Keena's sobs.

"Lux had a list of clients who she'd call any time you went out of town away on business. She would hold a small party so that we could entertain them and make some money on the side."

"Some money on the side, huh? So, you bitches was running y'all own operation and stealing from me?"

"Technically, it's not stealing because-" Before Naima could finish her statement, Charmaine jumped out of her chair and grabbed Naima by the neck while gritting her teeth.

"It is stealing if you are using my resources and I don't get a cut out of it. Dumb ass lil girl." Char returned back to her seat and set her eyes on Dahlia.

"Why were you in jail?"

"The hotel cameras picked up on me being the last person with Lux and they brought me in for questioning. I just told them we were good friends and we had drinks at the bar. After that, I don't know where she went. The cameras confirmed my story. They offered their condolences and let me go." Dahlia answered. Charmaine chuckled and rolled her eyes.

"They just let you go, huh? You really think it's as simple as that? THINK! They're gonna be watching you now, watching me! Look, I'm pulling in the reins. Nobody comes in or out of this building for a month. No clients, no nothing. And whatever the fuck y'all had going on behind my back, shut that shit down

NOW!" The girls stood in silence. They each looked around at one another as Charmaine continued to ramble on. "As a matter of fact, y'all gotta go. Go pack up them rooms and get the fuck out. Fuck around and blow my whole operation up." Charmaine spat. She was met with gasps and sighs. Charmaine was a pissed ball of nerves and it showed. In the midst of the drama, Dahlia remembered she needed to find out where Lenox's sister was, and she could not do that if Charmaine fired them all. Dahlia spoke up.

"Charmaine, I know we were wrong and out of line. We just went with the flow of things because we knew you left Lux in charge. I can't speak for Keena and Naima, but I'm sorry and I want to continue to work under you and learn to be a businesswoman like you." Charmaine paused and glared at each of the girls before finally agreeing to let them stay and work. She kept her word about them not seeing clients for a month, but as far as bringing in some sort of cash, she allowed them to be bottle girls at her strip club until things blew over with Lux.

Over the next month, each of the girls grieved Lux in different ways. Although Naima was closest to her, Keena seemingly took it the hardest. Without a doubt, Dahlia missed Lux, and the warehouse reminded her of that. She hated the lockdown more than anyone.

Chapter Fourteen

Dahlia felt like her plans to get back into culinary school were derailed. With Charmaine stopping their real cash flow, she was not able to stack like she intended. She had enough for at least one semester, but she had two semesters left before graduating. With the little she had saved, she would not be able to cover the semesters and a place to stay. The tips she made from working in the strip club were not nearly enough. She could not wait for Charmaine to give them the green light to work again. To kill time, she spent Wednesdays through Saturdays at the club, which in turn meant she didn't have much time for Lenox. She didn't mind not having much time with him because she had no new information regarding his sister. Furthermore, their relationship had been a little rocky since she was now aware that he was working with the FBI.

This day at the club was like any other. The atmosphere was dope. The purple, blue and pink lights filled the room. The music blared over the speakers, and the girls rolled their bodies because their bag depended on it. Naima and Dahlia had to learn to adapt to the scene. This was a different caliber of guests than the ones they were used to. Dope boys, young niggas, and bi-curious women filled the club. They often had difficulty keeping their hands to themselves. Keena, on the other hand, was in her element. They even called her on the stage once for *"Throwback Thursday"*. Keena easily made $1,000 that night. She was a crowd favorite and in her zone, making her coins.

Dahlia applied a coat of lipgloss to her lips, and propped her breasts up in her black crop top before taking the sizzling bottles to the VIP section. She stood at the table and presented the guests with their drinks.

"Can I get you boys anything else?" She asked, chewing her gum and flirting with her eyes.

"Yo number." One of the guys responded while pulling Dahlia onto his lap. It was the same shit every night. Being flirted with and fondled by random nobodies. Dahlia smiled and wiggled out of his grasp.

"Make sure you guys keep an eye on ya boy. It looks like he's already had enough to drink." She smiled. The guy pulled her back on his lap and licked her neck.

"How about a dance, baby?" His friends laughed. Before Dahlia could respond, Lenox yanked her off of him, grabbed the guy by his shirt, and slammed him onto the table. The bottles hit the ground and, while everybody was laughing a few minutes ago, they were quiet now. BG pulled a chair up, took a handful of the pretzels that were on the table, and tossed them in his mouth one by one.

"You need a lesson on keeping your hands to yo self, lil nigga?"

"My bad, Smoke, I-I ain't know that was yo girl." He begged with his hands up. "Come on, man, I'm getting married tomorrow." Lenox pulled out his gun and pressed it to the guy's forehead.

"Keep yo muthafuckin hands to yoself. Don't look her way, don't sniff her way, matter fact, don't bring yo ass back up here. Get the fuck out." The guy and his boys scurried away while Dahlia hurried to clean the mess that Lenox had just made. There was always some sort of drama going on in the club, so none of the other partygoers around them seemed to notice the chaos that had been unfolding. After Dahlia cleaned the section up, she followed Lenox outside to his car.

"I haven't seen you in two weeks and, the first time I do see you, you got on these little ass shorts, and some nigga got his hands on you. I thought we had an understanding?"

"Charmaine is on our ass after what happened to Lux. You asked me to find out where your sister is. I have to play the role. You cannot be showing up and starting fights. That's gon get me sent up! So back off, give me some damn space, Lenox."

"You **my** woman, fuck you mean give you some space? I ain't know we was gon run into you tonight. BG wanted to meet up here. Look, I'm not gon keep playing these games with you, Dahlia. I love you, I wanna be with you, and I can take care of you. You don't need this shit. Fuck what I said before about Charmaine. I told you I'mma find out what happened to my sister regardless. You need to tell her TONIGHT that you are done with this shit."

"I wanna be with you, too, but your sister is the priority. In order to get some information, you gotta chill and let me do this. Yeah, you can do it on your own, but you can get things done quicker with an inside tip. And to be honest, I need the money, Lenox. You encouraged me to finish school. There are certain steps I need to take to get there. Making sure I secure the bag is one of them."

"If money is the issue, I can take care of that for you."

"I need to do this on my own. I appreciate you wanting to help, but I need my own money."

"Can you get away tonight?" He asked, pulling her close to him.

"Probably not, but Sunday, I'll try to slip away." Lenox was still not too excited about not seeing her all day, every day. Still, he figured they could save that argument for another time.

"Aight, cool. On your way back in, can you let BG know that I'm ready to roll?" Dahlia agreed then kissed Lenox before turning away. She watched as he walked to his car then headed back into the club. She found BG still in the area in which they had left him.

"Hey, BG. Lenox said he is ready, and you can meet him at the car."

"How you feeling, shorty?"

"I'm fine. I know how to deal with these niggas. I grew up in Brainerd Park." She laughed.

"Naw, I mean how you feel knowing you got my nigga nose wide open? I told that nigga not to wife a ho."

"What did you just say to me?"

"Shiddd, I mean if the shoe fits. I tried to tell him about you. I told him about that luau shit and even got him up here tonight so he could catch you in action. But he ain't tryna hear shit I got say. That nigga got dreams of living a certain lifestyle and think you're his gateway into it. But I know the real him. The nigga name is Smoke for a reason. He's a beast, and he was one inch from bringing the savage out tonight. Let him do what he gon do. We got money to make out here and you in the way. Just fall back shorty, If you want what's best for him. The streets respect him. If they find out he bagging you, they'll take him for a joke. Ain't good for business, baby girl."

Dahlia was caught off guard by BG comments. But if it was one thing she learned in the streets of Chicago, neva let anyone see you sweat. "Am I coming between the little boy crush you have on him? It sounds like you admire him and want him all to yourself, BG. Believe this, just as serious as he is about me, I'm ten times more serious about him. I ain't gon let you or nobody else come between what we're trying to build. Now, you fall back. CLOWN!"

Dahlia brushed past BG and headed back into the club to finish her night. No lie, she was stuck on BG's words for a while. She wondered if she was really holding Lenox back from taking care of business. She pondered on if she should tell Lenox what BG said. It could go one of two ways: he could take BG's side over hers or take her side but lose BG in the process. It was one thing Dahlia knew about jealous folks-- they would stop at nothing to tear you down. Though the saying was '*keep your friends close and keep your enemies closer*'. Dahlia knew that, in this case, BG should be kept closer to Lenox.

***

Lenox and BG rode in silence. BG knew that when Lenox was quiet like this, he had shit on his mind. And because BG was a simple ass nigga, he tried to play on it.

"Bro, shorty gon get you sent up. You moved to New York to get yourself together and away from the streets. You were too close to bringing the goon out tonight. And shid, I'm all for it, especially if that means we getting back to the money. But what you did was reckless."

"Dahlia ain't have nothing to do with what happened tonight, bro."

"How come she didn't? She letting them niggas touch all over her. Them niggas is regulars; that wasn't their first time trying her. Shiddd, they gon keep coming back just to see if she gon fold. And for the right price, she might."

"Aye, bro, you're done speaking on my woman. She is solid, without a doubt. And I don't have to prove that shit to you. Let it go."

"Word?"

"Straight up." Lenox replied. Lenox and BG never got into each other's business when it came to relationships, so Lenox couldn't understand why he was so invested in his relationship with Dahlia.

Chapter Fifteen

Dahlia arrived at the hooters in Lansing, where Keena had just dropped her off. Keena had to make a run to River Oaks Mall, so Dahlia hitched a ride to meet Lenox for a quick lunch. When she walked in, he was seated and already had her bone in three mile island wings and curly fries waiting on her. Lenox knew the lockdown situation and was willing to take whatever time he had with her, even if it was just for a moment. Dahlia spoke and sat down, avoiding all eye contact with Lenox. She ate her wings, one after the other, and made no conversation with Lenox.

She did her best to ignore the shit BG said the other day, but it weighed heavy on her. Dahlia didn't want to be a burden on anyone, nor did she want to be the one keeping Lenox from finding out the truth about his sister. She knew breaking up with him would damage his heart and hurt her soul, but she had to do it.

"You okay?" Lenox finally asked while Dahlia finished her last curly fry.

"I've been meaning to tell you. I spoke with my advisor last week at Washburn. And he was telling me that I was chosen for their program to study abroad for a semester or two. The only issue is, it's in Italy."

"Word? That's dope." He said, wiping his hands with the towelette.

"Yeah, so...I was um, thinking about going for it. I can come out on top because they're willing to cover the tuition for those semesters. The hostel would be paid for and the only thing I would really be responsible for is my flight."

"That's what's up, so what you waiting on? Sounds like a solid opportunity. Do you need me to pay for your flight?"

"Honestly, I'm waiting for you to tell me not to go."

"Why would I do that, Dahlia?"

"Because we're building something. Why would you be willing to put that on the line?"

"Dahlia, this is your career we're talking about. Your future." The waitress came back to the table and left the bill there. She cleared the dishes while Lenox tried to figure out Dahlia's thought process.

"But it can put our relationship on hold for almost half a year."

"And I'll still be around when you get back, Dahlia. Ion know much about that culinary shit, but I do know you have a peace about yourself when you are cooking. We gon be good, no doubt. Don't miss out on this; you gotta go."

"And what about finding your sister?"

"I was investigating her disappearance before you came into my life. I'll be good, bae."

"You really trying to push me away?" Dahlia pulled out her phone and texted Keena to circle back and pick her up. She grabbed her purse and stood up from the table. Lenox watched her curiously, trying to figure out where they just went wrong. He put a $50 bill on the table and followed her out of the restaurant. They stood in the parking lot, Lenox still trying to figure out the issue. He tugged her arm.

"Push you away? Dahlia, are you serious?"

"Dead serious! What type of man would be okay with his woman going across the country?" She blurted out.

"What kind of man would be okay with his woman not following her dreams?" He retorted. "I will never be the nigga to stand in your way, and you shouldn't want me to."

"But you gotta stand for something, Lenox! Fuck this shit. I knew you was playing me from the start."

"Yo, you really tripping. Why are you doing this?"

"No, why are YOU doing this? I don't fit into your life, Lenox. I see that now. If you're willing to go six months without seeing me, then we aren't as in love as I thought."

"If you're scared to go, or scared to move forward in our relationship, just say that! You won't make me feel bad about supporting your decisions! What type of shit is that?"

"Bye, Lenox!" She said, noting Keena pulling up.

"Bye?"

"YES, BYE!" Dahlia shouted. "I'm good on you!" Dahlia jumped into Keena's front seat, slamming the door. She was fuming for many reasons. Fuming because she felt dismissed by Lenox, and fuming because she let BG get inside her head enough to ruin her relationship.

"What happened, girl? That was quick." Keena said.

"Nothing, just another day with another nigga."

"Y'all broke up?"

"I guess so." Dahlia said, looking out the window. She appreciated how supportive Lenox was. Hearing him encourage her to go was music to her ears. He was exactly the man she wanted him to be. But BG's words were indelibly marked on her brain. She knew he'd either spend his time making sure she was good overseas, or be crazy enough to follow her. Both of which would take him away from getting the truth about his sister. The only way Dahlia knew to keep him on track was ending their relationship- no matter how much it hurt her.

Keena was happy to have a front-row seat to Lia's drama. It was hard getting information to BG since Dahlia was so secretive. Although Keena didn't have much to go off, she got the gist: she and her guy were done. This meant that BG could stop worrying about her and pay more attention to Keena. She dropped Dahlia off and headed to see her man.

***

"So, update me. What's the latest on ya girl?" BG asked.

"What girl?" Keena asked, genuinely confused. Keena stood at the kitchen counter with boy shorts on and a pink tank top. She floured the chicken and dropped it into the grease. She added shredded cheese to her mac and cheese and poured it into a baking dish before sprinkling more cheese over the top

"The new girl."

"Lia?" She questioned, rolling her eyes. "Why are you so interested in her?"

"I'm not." he lied.. Keena put the macaroni and cheese in the oven and slammed it shut.

"We just finished doing all that fucking. I'm in your kitchen sweating, making macaroni and shit! The first thing you do is ask me something about another bitch?"

"Look, I said I'm not interested in her."

"Shit, I can't tell. Every time I turn around, you ask me questions about her. How would you feel if I asked you about another nigga every time you saw me?"

"I wouldn't feel shit cuz that wouldn't happen."

"And why not?"

"Cuz I'd whoop yo ass that's why. You need to chill. I told you I'm tryna make sure she is top notch for my guy."

"That doesn't mean that you can use all of OUR time together, talking about her. I am the most important person in your life right now, BG."

BG burst out in laughter. He laughed so loud that Keena almost cried. His eyes filled with tears and he began to choke from laughing so hard at her ridiculous comment. He couldn't fathom how Keena thought she was top-notch. Sure, she was a beautiful girl and gave the best top, but she was just another pretty face with nothing to offer.

"How you figure you're the most important person in my life?" He asked, still grinning and trying to compose himself.

"Because I'm pregnant, BG, and I'm keeping it. So, you can stop talking to me about Lia. Whoever she fucking is her business. Me and this baby are YOUR business. And we are not going anywhere; count on that." Keena was tired of her man talking about another woman. She wasn't one to hold her tongue, no matter who she was talking to. Keena awaited his response. Instead, he just stood to his feet and stared at her.

"No you not." He said, looking her up and down after finally composing himself.

"Oh yes, the fuck I am. I'm a good woman, and I'mma be an even better mother. I don't need anything from you or nobody else. So, if you don't wanna fuck with me no more, that's fine. I'll live. Real bitches always do. But what you are not gon do is discuss another girl every time you are in my presence. That's ova with. You're done playing in my face".

BG watched Keena turn the chicken and stir the green beans as if she didn't just blow his world up with the baby news. Quite honestly, a piece of him was actually excited to have a baby.

Chapter Sixteen

BG sat in the comfy chair, awaiting his meeting to start. It was unlike him to be meeting in the open like this, but he had some information to get off his chest.

"What's up, Ma Dukes?" He greeted when Charmaine finally entered her office.

"Why are you meeting me at the warehouse *at my office*, son? We can't risk Lia or anyone knowing we're related. Don't get sloppy on me now. There's already too much drama going on."

"Right. Speaking of Lia, we got a problem or two."

"If we got a problem, then you're not on your shit. That's why you're here, to make sure these problems that you speak of don't arise. What could possibly be the issue?" Charmaine asked, staring her son in the face.

"Well, for one, Keena is pregnant. I ain't mad, though. I kind of dig her a little." He said, smiling and rubbing his chin.

"I'm too young and damn sure too fine to be a grandmother. And I don't want a loose girl like that being the mother of my grandchildren."

"Dang ma, I thought you liked Keena."

"She from the west side, that's already a red flag. Ain't shit to like about her. Get rid of it."

"What about my happiness?" He laughed.

"You just inherited your father's empire. That's all the happiness you need."

"Aight but for real, ma, Lia working with the Law now. Yup, they pulled her in and threatened her with pops and Lux murder, so now she cooperating with them. You should have just let me do that shit. You left a trail when you did it at his hotel room."

"That was personal, son. I had to do it myself. Sick of your father promising these lil bitches the world. Promising to give them the shit I helped him build! Did you know he planned on marrying her? That would have stopped the cash flow for everything I got going on. How do you know all this anyway?"

"Smoke and Keena."

"Lenox told you all this? Now, that, I don't believe." She said while watering her plants.

"Hell naw, he didn't. I told you how that nigga is. I just had to put two and two together. Everything he left out was filled in by Keena. You know shorty just be bumping her gums. And you know what else, even though Smoke ain't said much, I believe he's still looking for his sister, too."

Charmaine shrugged and lit a cigarette. "Another lil bitch who Black promised the world to. That's who you should have let me take care of. She thought that because she was screwing your father, she would tell me what she was and wasn't going to do. These young girls have no respect!"

"Naw, ma, that was personal for me. But that shit ova with, dead, buried. So what are we going to do about Lia? Smoke listens to anything that bitch has to say, he ride so hard for her. It's only a matter of time before she put a bug in his ear about me."

Charmaine leaned back in her chair, took a pull from her cigarette, and blew a frustrated cloud of smoke into the air. Charmaine was hoping Lia would be her protege. She was beautiful, smart, and loyal. Unfortunately for her, she was loyal to the wrong person.

"Get rid of her." Char replied. BG nodded and left his mother's office. That was the greenlight he needed. Dahlia was in the way. He was going to handle that without hesitation.

Because of the conversation she had just had with BG, Char was now in her feelings. Char was once a sweet and loyal young girl with a heart of gold. She married Black at the young age of 18. She was easily wooed by the man who was ten years her senior. The glitz, glam, and many properties he had made up for the verbal and emotional abuse she endured, as well as him staying away for weeks at a time. Charmaine was loyal to Black over the years, even when he mistreated their son. *If only she could make him love her*, she thought. Charmaine did everything she could to show she was worthy of his love. She started the Suga Baby strip club and escort business to add more money to his empire, and he had the nerve to ask her for a divorce so he could run off with one of her employees! The fact that Dani was screwing Black under her nose sent Charmaine over the edge, so she made sure BG dealt with her. And now he thought he was going to do the same thing with Lux.

"Over my dead body or his." She said out loud. That sweet young girl turned into a bitter 45-year-old woman hellbent on taking what was hers. That's why when she met them in that hotel room, she had no problem putting a bullet to his dome. And Lux was a weak bitch, which is why she shoved the Pink Ladie Pills down her throat. Lux was a casualty of war which was a shame. She was Char's favorite.

BG left his mother's office on a mission. From the outside looking in, Black Greystone, Charmaine, and BG were strangers to each other. No one knew the oil tycoon had a family that he didn't give two fucks about, and that's how Charmaine meant to keep it.

BG never forgave his namesake for the many affairs he had over the years on his mother or the abuse he put him and his mother through. And, even though Black flipped the script and changed his ways in the end, BG didn't give two fucks if the nigga was breathing or not. His feelings about his dad had to be put aside because his mother had finally given him the green light to get rid of Dahlia. And he was definitely going to enjoy that.

Chapter Seventeen

Between losing Lux and purposely letting go of Lenox, Dahlia was just...sad. Although she and Lux started off rocky, she grew to really like her. She got used to her cozy lifestyle and seeing her every day, adjusting to her being gone proved to be more difficult than expected. What made matters worse was that she fell for Lenox harder than she imagined she would. But she threw the relationship away, and why? Because his extra jealous best friend had a boy crush on him? The more she thought about it, the more foolish she felt for breaking up with him. She wanted to lay in her bed, wallowing in her grief, but it was Halloween, and she had plans.

"Hey boo, are you still coming to the Halloween joint with us tonight?" Keena asked, barging into Dahlia's room and plopping on her bed.

"Dang Keena, you need to perfect the art of knocking because that was beyond intrusive." Dahlia said, rolling her eyes. Dahlia opened the bag of Harold's Keena had brought her. She immediately indulged in her six-piece wings, fried hard with mild sauce, salt, and pepper.

"Girl, fuck all that. You ain't in here doing nothing, you coming or not?" Keena asked, dismissing Dahlia's feelings.

"Yeah, I'm coming. Naima is still coming too, right?" Dahlia asked

"Probably. She said she's not feeling good. So it may just be us mamas. And you know that don't make a difference to me cuz that's more money in my pocket, ya heard me?"

"You so silly, girl. Where is it again?" Dahlia asked, checking her phone for the tenth time to see if Lenox had called.

"Midway Airport."

"Girl, what?" Dahlia replied with a mouth full of fries.

"Yeah, remember my client owns a private plane. He is just trying to have some fun until takeoff." She said, sipping her grape Crush pop.

"Damn Keena, what kind of shit you got me involved in? You're telling me I gotta put on a costume just to sit on a little ass plane"-

"And have drinks, bitch, yes! What's the problem? It's two stacks in it for both of us." Keena chimed in. "If you miss that nigga, just say that." She laughed.

"We in and out, girl. I wanna make sure we make the booze cruise later. All we do is work, and I wanna have some fun for a change. And no, I don't miss anyone." Dahlia lied.

"We'll make the booze cruise, don't worry!"

Keena retired to her room to rest before the night's events. Around 5:30, the girls both started to get ready. Keena settled on a sexy nurse outfit. The little white dress, sexy red heels, and stethoscope around her neck would have sent any man to the emergency room. Keena was to die for while Dahlia played it safe as always. She put on a Chucky costume, applied some red lipstick to her lips, and called it a day. They knocked on Naima's door before leaving to check in with her, but she didn't answer. They assumed she decided to stay in and left without her. Keena drove to Midway Airport and parked in the garage. They took a secret route to one of the private hangars where the jet party was.

When they got to the charter plane, the staircase was extended. There was a black Escalade with dark tints parked next to the jet, and a red carpet rolled out for the guests. Dahlia looked in the tinted windows attempting to fix her hair and apply gloss to her lipstick before heading into the plane.

"Keena, my hair is stuck in my necklace. Can you pull it out for me? I can't see." Dahlia whined. Keena swiftly removed her hair from her necklace.

"I'm sorry." Keena said.

"For wha"- Before Dahlia could finish the question, Keena had already injected her with the needle BG had given to her prior to their arrival. Dahlia's body fell into the door, then to the concrete. Suddenly, BG got out of the truck.

"Damn, baby! I didn't think you had it in you." He said, clapping his hands.

"I told you I'll do anything for you, baby." Keena said. Keena watched as BG's security carried Dahlia's body onto the charter. She rubbed her belly, feeling the baby's fluttering kick for the first time. Which reminded her, BG made her a promise that they would discuss the baby. "Bae, where are you taking her? Don't forget you said we could talk about the baby."

"Oh yeah, that's right," he said, turning around. **POW POW** "I don't want a baby." BG said after he put a bullet to her belly and her dome. Keena's nurse costume filled with blood while her body hit the wet concrete. BG's security put her in the Escalade and drove off. BG walked with his head held high onto his plane. He smiled and took a deep breath. He finally had the one thing he'd wanted for the last six months- the black barbie.....Dahlia.

Chapter Eighteen

Dahlia's neck ached once she finally awoke. She looked around at her grand surroundings. A beautiful chandelier hung on the ceiling above her, and arched, floor-to-ceiling windows surrounded her. She found herself sitting at a long dinner table with a large spread including rolls, wine, different cheeses and grapes.

"Good, you're awake!" BG said, snapping Dahlia into awareness. "Girls, I want you to meet Lia. Lia, this is Laci and Ashley." He said, pointing at two girls on one side of the table. He walked over to another woman on the opposite side of the table. "And this is my wife." He said, pointing to the young woman. "Ladies, Lia is going to be spending some time with us. I want you to make her feel at home."

"Welcome, Lia." They all said in unison.

Though the women smiled and spoke, they concentrated on avoiding all eye contact with her. Dahlia was confused. She didn't know where she was or who any of the people were besides BG. She stood up, completely over the weird Stepford Wives scene.

"Is this some kind of a joke? BG, I don't know what game you're playing, but you need to take me home.

Yo life is already on the line, yo boy not going for this shit, I'm sure you know that" she said.

"Take you home?" He laughed. "Sit yo ass down before I make you sit down, and that you do not want me to do, trust me. My butler prepared a decent meal for us to enjoy together as a family. Might be a while before the drugs wear off, and the shit I gave you can have some nasty side effects if you don't have something on your stomach." He warned.

Dahlia eased back into her chair and sat in complete silence while her mind raced against time. BG and the other ladies engaged in casual conversation as if she was not sitting there at the table with them. Dahlia glared at all the women. She noticed a familiar face when her heart stopped in horror. At first glance, Dahlia couldn't recognize her because she appeared quite the opposite of how she was previously described. But sure enough, it was Dani. Lenox described her as strong-willed and outgoing. Dahlia recalled seeing her picture on his bookcase. Dani was beautiful, vibrant, and filled with life. But sitting at the table before her, she was a shell of what he described and nothing how Dahlia imagined her. She looked tired, probably a result of being under BG for almost a year.

 Dahlia was afraid of what was to come next. She didn't know if BG would starve her or if she would muster up enough courage to escape. Either way, he was right. She did need her strength, especially since whatever he drugged her with was weighing her down. Her legs were weak, and she felt groggy. After listening to their conversation and watching them eat, Dahlia decided to try some of the food placed in front of her by the servers. She nibbled on a piece of bread and took a couple of spoonfuls of soup. She looked at the asparagus placed before her and remembered her and Lenox's argument over if it makes your pee smell or not.

BG got up from his end of the table and walked over to Dahlia. He placed his hands on her shoulders and slid them down to her breast.

"We're going to have a lot of fun." He said. Dahlia took her fork and jabbed him in his arm.

"Don't touch me CLOWN!" She spat, silencing the entire room.

"ARGH BITCH!" he said, backhanding her, sending her weak body to the floor. BG picked Dahlia up by her neck and slammed her on the table. The dishes clattered, sending chills and pain down Dahlia's spine. Dani sat expressionlessly and continued eating her food, as did the other ladies. With Dahlia pinned to the table, BG whispered in her ear. "Smoke might have let you get away with that attitude, but that shit won't fly here. Disrespect me again if you think I'm bullshitting." He said, finally letting her neck go.

"Baby, show our guest to her room." He demanded while wiping the corn soup from his clothing. Dahlia held back her tears and focused on catching her breath. *Don't let him see you sweat,* she said to herself. She gathered herself as the maids around her scurried to pick up the dishes and clean the mess.

"Come on, Lia." Dani said. Dahlia followed her through the massive home until they got to what appeared to be her room. "If you resist him, it'll only get worse." Dani said.

"Dani, has he told you about me?"

"Nothing to tell. BG always brings other women home. As long as he's safe, I don't care." Dahlia was puzzled. Dani spoke as if they were in a relationship. It was either that or a weird Stockholm Syndrome situation going on.

"Do you want to be here, Dani?"

"You keep calling me Dani like you know me, and you don't. You just another bitch along for the ride. He'll break you off with some money when he's done with you. So stop acting like we are friends or family. We're far from that."

"Dani, your brother Lenox is my boyfriend." Dahlia was met with a long pause. She didn't understand the silence. She was sure that mentioning Lenox would put a smile on Dani's face, but she stood expressionless.

"Then why are you here?" She asked flatly.

"Do I look like I wanna be here? Hell, it don't even look like YOU wanna be here. He abducted me, and I'm sure he did the same to you. Lenox told me you couldn't stand BG, so I don't buy this loyal girlfriend act you're putting on now. BG is a creep. He's a fucking snake, but he's not as smart as he thinks he is. Lenox is going to come for me. I can guarantee you that. And when he does, and he sees you, his heart is gonna explode. He's been looking for you since you left. I mean, ACTIVELY searching for you, Dani."

Dahlia searched Daniella's face but found nothing. Whatever it was that had happened to her over the past year must have been tough because she showed no signs of emotion. Daniella finally broke the silence.

"I put some fresh towels in the bathroom for you. My room is down the hall, his is on the other side of the villa. Should you need anything, you can let me or the staff know."

"What happened to you? Your brother never gave up on you; why are you giving up on yourself?" Dahlia asked in frustration.

"Have a good night, Lia." She responded, dismissing Dahlia again. "BG likes to have breakfast on the terrace every morning. I'll see you then."

When Dani left the room, Dahlia looked around. Everything was a reminder that it was his mansion they were in. The throw pillows on the bed had the letters B.G stitched into them. Even one of the fire pokers in the set next to the fireplace had the letters B.G on it. The man was clearly full of himself. His arrogance in keeping his bestfriends sister added to the disgust Dahlia already felt about him. She fell asleep terrified that night. It was clear BG was missing a few screws and had no issue being violent. Her neck was sore and her face ached due to the pain inflicted on her by him. And, although she moved a dresser in front of the door to keep BG from coming in, she still tossed and turned all night.

***

Dahlia woke up the next morning and contemplated her next move. She felt as if it would be in her best interest to go along with whatever BG had up his sleeve until Lenox arrived- if Lenox arrived. Because at the same time, she wasn't so sure that he'd show. Dahlia pushed him away, so he's probably unaware that she's missing. More importantly, as smart and thorough as Lenox was, his best friend held his sister captive for almost a year, and he had no clue. Now that was the most terrifying thought of all.

Dahlia heard a knock at her door and hurried over to remove the dresser from in front of it. When she opened the door, she found Dani standing there. She told her breakfast would be served on the terrace in 15 minutes. She handed her a white dress and told her she must wear that to breakfast. After showering, combing her hair into a curly bun, and oiling her body, she hesitantly headed out of her "room". She took in the beautiful space she was in before heading down the grand, spiral staircase. She had not paid much attention to her surroundings last night, but this Spanish-styled home had a grand foyer that complemented the luxury around it. Dahlia quickly surveyed the room for a phone but was unsuccessful. She spotted Dani, who stood directing her out to the terrace.

Dahlia and Dani sat at the table without speaking to one another. Birds chirped around them, and the greenery was plentiful and lush. The grandiosity of the villa and the peacefulness of the terrace itself was something out of a home and garden magazine. Unfortunately, it was Dahlia's personal hell, and even worse, the Devil himself had just arrived. BG kissed both of them on the forehead - which made Dahlia's skin crawl and stomach turn. He then sat to have breakfast with his ladies.

The servers poured mimosas and sat a buffet of croissants, fruit, eggs, and sausages before them. BG piled his plate with no hesitation. Dani put a croissant on her plate with eggs and a piece of cantaloupe.

"You can put that croissant back; you're getting a little too heavy for me." BG said. Dani put the croissant back onto the platter and sipped her mimosa, very unbothered by his comment. Dahlia shook her head and rolled her eyes.

"You should eat. You're gonna want to keep your strength because I have a surprise for you. Smoke will be here any day now." BG noted how Dahlia's face lit up with joy and he kept talking. "Yeah, he was so broken up about you leaving him that I invited him here to take his mind off of you."

"What do you mean he was broken up about me leaving him?"

"Oh, Keena told me you broke up with him over some bullshit. So you, well *I* - sent him a text from your phone saying you decided to study culinary abroad in Italy and that your flight was leaving in the morning." BG looked at his watch. So, according to the time, you've been in Italy for about....twelve hours now. You ain't let him know you made it or nothing. That's crazy." BG taunted.

"I told him I was going. But he'll never believe that I left without personally saying goodbye." Dahlia stated with tears filling her eyes.

"He already does, especially after you broke his heart at Hooters that day. At this point, it looks like you're capable of anything. So, anyway. My boy gon fly out in a couple of days. He's going to stay at a hotel, and then he's gonna swing by here. I'mma hook him up with some girls, and soon he'll forget all about you.

"BG, why are you doing this? Why take everything he loves? Me, his sister?" When Dahlia mentioned Dani being Lenox's sister, he scowled at Dani as if she'd let out the big secret. "She didn't say anything," Dahlia added. "You have her too tightly wrapped around your finger. He's supposed to be your best friend. I knew you was a snake."

"Lenox gets whatever he wants. You were supposed to be mine, Dahlia. You think him spilling his drink on you was an accident? I mean, it was, but he spilled it because he was so thirsty to get your number before I did. He broke his neck to get to you. But it's okay; I got you now." He smiled

The only thing more satisfying to BG other than having two of Lenox's favorite girls with him was having them under the same roof as Lenox without Lenox's knowledge. BG had a weird competition complex going on with Lenox. Ever since they met on the streets, then ended up at the same high school, BG felt he had to compete. The girls wanted Lenox, and the streets feared him. He was always in Lenox's shadow, but that was soon to change. Once he realized that Dahlia wasn't returning, he was certain Lenox would head back to New York to live out the rest of his pathetic life. A life without family or anyone to love.

"I hope your 'wife' knows that you been fucking Keena all this time. Thats the only logical explanation for her setting me up for you."Enraged, Dahlia stood up and flipped the table. The mimosas, the food, all landed on BG and Dani. Dani stood up, ready to attack Dahlia, but BG held her back, while whispering something in her ear. Shortly after Dani escorted Dahlia back to her room. This only infuriated her more. The door was locked from the inside with no way for Dahlia to get out. She paced back and forth as time crept past her. After hours and hours of her mind racing, and attempts to come up with plans, the sun set and It was soon night. Dahlia realized she hadn't eaten since the breakfast debacle earlier that day, nor had she seen another human life.

It was clear that Dahlia had more fight in her than BG expected. When he visited her the following morning she was pacing back and forth, which he watched her do all night through the camera he had hidden in there. "Lia" he said. Dahlia continued to pace, ignoring him. "Lia"

"My name is Dahlia! You don't get to call me anything other than that. I'm not your woman! And I'm not your friend" She yelled!

BG ignored the mini tantrum and stared at her. "I'm giving you some of the best hospitality, Lia, but you've been behaving in a disrespectful, ungrateful manner."

"Does that hurt your feelings?" She asked sarcastically. "I don't care what you do. I'll never be one of these pathetic bitches in here!" She yelled. Dahlia paced back and forth. It wasn't the lack of meals that was starting to get to her—it was the idea of being trapped with BG forever.

BG glared at Dahlia. His blood was boiling, and he was losing his patience with her. He thought that locking her in her room all day would get him some sort of results, but it didn't. So, the next day, he tried making her skip a few meals and then limiting her portions whenever she did eat—still nothing. He was sure that food deprivation would weaken her mind. However,, there were two things he didn't know. He didn't realize Dahlia had spent months in her car, so missing a meal wasn't out of the norm for her. Secondly, he didn't know that Dahlia was patiently waiting for Lenox to arrive. She had her own plan on how to help him figure out she was there. In her mind, she was standing firm. She didn't realize BG was a ticking time bomb about to explode.

Dahlia's living conditions had gotten worse. At this point, BG left her in her room with a sheet and turned the heat off. Dahlia used the matches by the fireplace and lit a fire to stay warm. She prayed and hoped that she was in a dream, that her life had not taken this drastic turn. For the first time since her grandmother died, she cried herself to sleep. Meanwhile on the other side of the villa, Dahlia was the topic of conversation.

"How long are we going to do this, play this game?"

"Don't start, Dani. We're only in this situation because you were too afraid to tell Smoke we was together."

"No, we're only in this because you was scared to tell your mother we were dating. Then you lied and had her thinking I was sleeping with Black! She tried to get you to kill me. All of this is your fault, BG."

"And now I have to sit here day after day with no connection to the outside world. I have to watch you bring your new flavor of the month in here, and I'm supposed to be okay with it? Who the hell do you think you are, Casanova? And what the hell did she mean when she brought up Keena? I know you wasn't messing around with that nasty bitch."

"Bae, don't listen to her. And trust me, Dahlia will be the last girl I bring in, I promise."

"What's your obsession with her BG?"

"What do you mean?"

"I mean, if she's my brother's girlfriend like she claims to be, what do *you* want with her? That's triflin."

"I thought you hated him because he took your parents away from you? I'm getting this revenge for you, baby. I'm taking everything he loves so he can suffer just like you've suffered without your parents."

BG thought about the day Dani came home to her parents' house being on fire.

Lenox's parents, Mr. and Mrs. LeBlanc, sat in the living room. Mrs. LeBlanc sat doing a crossword puzzle while Mr. LeBlanc watched the wheel of fortune. Lenox's mother headed to the door after hearing the bell ring. BG entered, greeting Mrs. LeBlanc with a kiss on the cheek and heading back to the den to have a discussion with Mr. LeBlanc. Shortly after, Lenox's father and BG got into a heated discussion. Mr. LeBlanc had a gambling problem that Lenox was unaware of, and he owed BG $45,000. When he couldn't settle his debt, he paid for it with his and his wife's lives. After using a silencer to put a bullet to both of their heads, he sat two chairs in the living room and placed their lifeless bodies in them before finally tying them up. Afterward, he took lighter fluid and doused their bodies in it, then set them ablaze.

BG ran out the back door and around to the front of the house to his car. Dani, who had just gotten out of her car, ran up to her childhood home that was now engulfed in flames. She screamed at the top of her lungs and collapsed in the arms of her parents' killer and love of her life. BG eventually told her that Lenox owed a Mexican gang leader some money and that's why they attacked the family. He made her keep it a secret and promised to help her get revenge. The lie she was unaware of tore her away from Lenox and, ultimately, destroyed their relationship. Dani never forgave her brother, who she thought was responsible for the death of their parents.

"I don't like how you dote on her." She said, snapping BG out of his daydream. "She's been disrespectful. You need to teach her a lesson. She needs to fall in line before them other hoes think they can test you too. You know what to do, bae." She said.

BG knew he had to stop coddling Lia before Dani became suspicious of his true feelings for her. So later that night, he paid Dahlia a visit.

***

Boom Boom BOOM!! Dahlia was awakened by her bedroom door being knocked down in the middle of the night. The moon shined brightly through her window as she jumped to her feet.

"Pin her down." She heard BG say in a calm, but frightening voice. Dahlia was bum-rushed by the girls, including Dani. She swung when she could, but she was overpowered by the three women who hit, kicked, and punched her. Dani pulled her hair and scratched her face before they all slammed her to the floor face first. Dahlia lay there panting, fighting to breathe and trying not to cry before she heard BGs voice again. "It didn't have to be this hard. I never planned to hurt you; I actually like you. You just need to be *tamed* a little, that's all." Dani took the straps down from Dahlia's spaghetti strapped shirt and sat on Dahlia's legs while the other two girls pinned her arms down to the side of her body. Dahlia's bare back was cold from the chill in the room, while her breasts were mushed into the floor.

She observed BG leaning against the mantle on the fireplace. Her eyes were wide with fear as she stared at him with an inkling of what was to come next. "Wait!" Dahlia pleaded, sniffling as the blood trickled from her nose. "I'm sorry." She said, slightly above a whisper, barely able to catch her breath. "BG, I'm sorry. Please give me another chance."

"You're not sorry, Dahlia, but you will be." He retorted.

A blood-curdling scream escaped Dahlia's mouth as the hot iron melted into her flesh. BG was dead set on making her suffer, making her submit, turning her into his property. Thus, he branded the letters BG into her skin, just below her shoulder.

Dahlia lay on the floor, panting heavily. Sweat had formed on her head, causing her hair to stick to her skin. In that moment, BG knew he had won. Dahlia whimpered and cried. She was finally broken. There was no need to lock the doors and restrain her because BG knew they had reached a point of no return. They left her to her misery, branded, sobbing alone in the dark.

Chapter Nineteen

After the love and support I gave her, I can't believe she played me like that, Lenox thought to himself. It had been at least a week since Dahlia broke up with him because he encouraged her to study abroad. *What kind of shit is that?* He thought, shaking his head. Then, for Dahlia to send him some bullshit text without coming to physically say goodbye only infuriated him more. He'd already blown up her phone and sent multiple texts to her, but she had yet to respond. Not only did he lose his girl, but he lost the only lead to finding his sister. So, when BG called, attempting to smooth things over and inviting him to his Villa in Mexico, he gladly accepted it.

Before Lenox hopped on the flight to Mexico, he decided to stop into the police station to let them know he would not be returning. He didn't see any reason to stick around after losing his girl, and the trail to his sister's case had turned cold.

"Lenox, I know we have had our differences, but I was truly hoping to help bring some closure about your sister." Agent Walker stated.

"It's okay. The truth will emerge one day. Meanwhile, I can't put my life on hold waiting for that to happen."

"That's right. You got that chocolate girl to keep you company." The agent laughed.

"One more thing," Lenox said, ignoring the agent's attempt to get in his business, "has there been any new information to arise that could bring Charmaine down?"

"I wish. Nothing is tied to her. The people who worked for her aren't talking. We don't know where her headquarters are exactly. And even if we did, we don't have justification for a search warrant. That's one smart woman."

"Yeah, she is." Lenox walked out of the police station and sat in his car. The thought of his parents' death, his missing sister, and now losing Dahlia had finally got to him. He hadn't shed a tear over any of his misfortunes until now. He cried, broke down, asked his creator for direction, forgiveness, and peace. Before long, his flight was underway on a private jet to Puerto Vallarta, Mexico. When the wheels landed on the runway, Lenox took a breath of fresh air. The goal was to have a good time and take a load off. But he knew that after this trip, he'd be done with BG and anything else that reminded him of Chicago.

***

"My nigga!! Welcome to paradise!" BG said, greeting his best friend and unbeknownst to Lenox, his nemesis- at the door of his villa. Lenox walked into the grand villa and was greeted by BG and two topless girls—Laci and Ashley. Lenox paid little mind to their round breasts and wide hips because there was only one woman for him. And with all the action around him, he still anticipated Dahlia's call even though she ignored all of his.

"You look tired, you good, bro?" BG asked.

"Yeah, I'm straight." Lenox said, shaking up with BG. Lenox's luggage was taken by one of the butlers. Lenox knew BG saved a lot of the money they made transporting guns, but he didn't know he was living like this. "Yo crib decent, bro."

"Gratitude! So, you ready to kick it or what?" BG asked.

"I'm just here to chill, foe. I ain't really in the mood for partying." Lenox shrugged.

"That's cuz you agonizing ova that bitch, but I'mma take care of you though." BG took a small bell out of his pocket and rang it. Shortly after, one of BG's maids approached- topless- with a tray that held six shots of Don Julio. Lenox and BG both took three shots each. After downing the shots, Lenox felt compelled to partake in the festivities BG laid out. Lenox thought he was chilling with BG like old times, but apparently, BG was throwing a bachelor party for some Mexican dude, and the party happened to be that night. There was an overflow of alcohol, women, and more women mixed with food, music, and inappropriate antics. The two old friends indulged in more alcohol as music blared over the speakers. BG had to admit, this was the Lenox he remembered and loved, but this was also the Lenox he envied and loathed. As the festivities went on, BG contemplated putting Lenox out of his misery. But every time he got ready to take his life, he relished the idea of Lenox's everlasting agony of a life without his sister and his lover, so he let the nigga breathe.

The night grew late, and at about two in the morning, when it seemed, the partying would cease to end, BG's guests started to trickle out. On the other hand, Lenox was drunk out of his mind, staring up at the ceiling from the bed as the two women took control of his body. Cheating on Dahlia was the last thing on his mind; in fact, SHE was the only thing on his mind. He longed for her soft lips on his chest and the scent of vanilla and honey from her hair tickling his nostrils when she would bury her head into his neck. It was clear that she wanted nothing to do with him, and he was willing to face the regret of his current decisions once he sobered up. But for now, he would surrender to the touch of the BBW before him.

On the other side of the villa, Dahlia and Dani was wide awake. Earlier, BG kept them in the room together to assure they didn't try anything funny with Lenox being there. In fact, it was the first time he'd ever locked Dani away, but he didn't want to risk anything. The girls said not one word to each other for the duration of the time they were together. But once the maid came to unlock the door, Dani attempted to leave but was stopped abruptly by Dahlia.

"Dani, I won't pretend to know what your relationship is like with BG. I just want to say that if you love him as much as I love Lenox, then I know you don't want to share him with anyone. And so, I need your help. I can't be here." Dahlia said with pleading eyes. "I don't want to be here. All I'm asking is for you to leave the door unlocked tomorrow morning. The rest I'll handle myself. BG will never have to know you helped me escape. Please?" She said, reaching out to Dani's hand. Dani pulled her hand back and exited Dahlia's room.

Moments after Dani left, BG entered Dahlia's room. It was his first time coming face to face with her since branding her. He was reluctant to admit it, but he actually felt bad for violating her like that- kind of. He wasn't a sadist; he preferred to taunt her in a different way, which is why the visit to her room tonight was a little different. The psychological games BG played were nothing short of how egomaniacal he was. Dahlia sat on the bed, hoping BG would stay far away from her. The closer he got, the more she cringed.

"Sweetheart, can I get you anything before I turn in for the night?" BG was met with silence, so he continued. "Lenox and I had a great time. He's almost back to his old self. I'm sure after tonight, you'll be nothing more than a fleeting memory."

Dahlia's eyes welled with tears, but she refused to let them fall. BG headed towards the door before torturing her one last time. "Bae, I noticed you haven't touched any of the books I left you. I thought "From Homies to Lovers by Jaz Akins", was one of your favorite books?" Still Dahlia said nothing. BG continued his game with her. "Well, at least watch some TV," he said. He turned the TV on and tossed the remote back to the bed where Dahlia was sitting. She stared at the television and the tears she tried so desperately to hold back fell from her eyes as she screamed at the top of her lungs. She threw the remote at the flatscreen over the fireplace. The screen shattered immediately, but that did nothing for the image she saw of Lenox and the two girls working their magic on him—an image that was now sketched in her brain. Dahlia tossed and turned the entire night, hoping his sister heard her plea earlier.

Dani went to sleep that night with a conflicted heart. She owed her loyalty to BG and nobody else. Lenox had betrayed her and their family, so why would she make his life easier by sending his girlfriend back to him? On the other hand, Dahlia was right. Dani was tired of sharing BG with everyone else. Letting Dahlia free would provide one less person for Dani to have to compete with. Dani didn't know what she would do, and only time would tell.

Chapter Twenty

Lenox woke the next morning with a massive headache, noticing two girls in the room with him. Once he came to himself, he sent the girls on their way. He must admit, BG still knew how to throw a party. Although the goal was to make him forget about Dahlia, he couldn't. Lenox called Dahlia two more times before rolling out of bed, but there was still no answer—straight to voicemail like before. He played their conversation over in his head and came up with nothing. She was genuinely pissed that he called himself supporting her dreams. Now, all he could do in his head was give her some space. He hoped she would come around before the distance killed them. Lenox meditated, showered, then headed downstairs. BG was sitting in the grand room as if he didn't drink as much liquor as Lenox did the night before.

"So, you had fun last night, huh?" BG asked.

"Man, that shit was a movie, no doubt. Thanks, bro, I needed that. I appreciate it. And no matter what you feel about Dahlia, she's good for me. She keeps me on track. I'mma give her some time, and she'll call me. I know she will."

"Look, bro, I'm only telling you this because we are family. Move on. If she can go all the way to Italy and not look back, then she doesn't deserve you."

"Nigga look at you tryna sound all caring and compassionate." Lenox said, following him out to the terrace. They sat at the table, awaiting their food to arrive. Lenox checked his flight itinerary, making sure he was good to go the next morning, while BG summoned the servers so they could eat. First, the server who resembled the woman that killed Selena brought Lenox out a plate of salmon and eggs benedict. Lenox immediately thought about the first night he and Dahlia spent together and how she made him breakfast the next day. BG scoffed down his food while Lenox picked at his. He was suddenly sick to his stomach at the thought that was forming in his brain. Suddenly, the Yolanda Saldivar lookalike brought out more food.

"Here you go, Senor. I hear you like cinnamon in your pancakes. Isn't that what your mother used to put in her batter?" She asked, placing the pancakes before him. Lenox's heart sank as he took his gun by the barrel. There was only one person who knew about the cinnamon: Dahlia. He reached over the table and grabbed BG by his shirt, catching him off guard. He pistol-whipped him, giving BG no time to breathe or react.

"Where the fuck is she?" Lenox barked.

"Bro, you're tripping," BG coughed while blood leaked from his mouth. "Where is who?"

"Dahlia! She would never leave without saying bye!" Lenox cocked the pistol and held it to BG's forehead. "SPEAK NIGGA!"

"Man, fuck you and that Bitch." BG retorted, pushing Lenox through the terrace window. Lenox landed on a pile of glass while BG pounced on him. BG reached for Lenox's gun, but Lenox wasn't letting him take him out before he found his woman. The best friends brawled, knocking over lamps, blood splashing here and there, but Lenox got the best of BG. The sound of a gun going off startled both BG, who was on the ground, and Lenox, who was on top of him with his gun now to his forehead again. Lenox looked up in disbelief.

"Dani?"

"Get off of him, Lenox!" Dani yelled, trembling while pointing the gun at her big brother. "Get off of him, now!" She exclaimed. Lenox removed the gun from BG's head and stood up. "Now, drop the gun," she demanded.

"Dani, you know I can't do that."

"Drop it!" She yelled. Lenox hesitantly but slowly put his gun on his waist. He held his hands up and continued to try to reason with his sister. His sister that he had not seen in *a year*. His sister, who he helped raise, babysat, loved, and protected, and *searched* for.

"I don't know what you're doing here, Dani, or what he has told you, but it's all been a lie."

"No, YOU lied! You lied, Lenox! Mom and dad would still be here if it wasn't for you!"

"Dani—" Lenox attempted to reason with her, but a shot rang out, shooting the vase next to him. BG was praying that Dani hurried up and shot Lenox so he wouldn't have to reveal the truth about him being the one to kill her parents. Although he envied Lenox and wanted him to lose everything, he loved Dani just as much. BG loved Dani with all his heart, and the thought of losing her or hurting her was terrifying.

"Shoot him, Dani! He took everything from you."

"Dani, what is it that you think I did?" Lenox begged for an answer from his little sister.

"You owed those Mexican people some money or stole from them. That's why they came after mom and dad."

It wasn't until this very moment that Lenox put all the pieces together. When he arrived at his parents' house that night, BG and Dani were already there. BG was apparently there first and told Lenox what he had seen. Lenox never once mentioned anything to Dani, and furthermore, she didn't know anything about his drugs and gun business. So why would she assume anything now?

"Dani, who told you that? BG? Dani, listen. Was BG there when you got to the house that night?" Dani recalled the night of the fire. She remembered BG running from the back of the house, and she swore she saw a car with the Mexican flag in it—because that's what BG told her. He told her the same story over and over, so it *had* to be true. Dani lowered the gun she had pointed at her brother. "Dani, was he there?" He paused, waiting for a response, but Dani was in deep thought. "Now, ask yourself *why* he was there?"

"Shoot that nigga, baby! He's a fucking liar!" BG blurted out. Without hesitation, Dani lifted her gun and shot Lenox in the shoulder. Dahlia screamed from the top of the stairs as she had just managed to pull herself out of bed. The adrenaline sent her flying to Lenox's side, seeing him cough up blood. His eyes were wide with confusion as Dahlia appeared before him. BG managed to stand to his feet and walked over to where Dani was. "Give me the gun and go upstairs, baby. I don't want you to see this."

"Baby, why were you at my parents' house?" Dani asked, tears falling from her eyes.

"Come on now, Dani, I was there to see you. You know this." Dani tried her best to recall the worst night of her life. From the moment she got off work to the moment her parents were put into the body bags.

"No, you weren't. The plan was to meet at the Soho House at 7:30 pm because you said you had to take care of some business. You didn't know I would be home, and no one knew we were dating, so you wouldn't have been bold enough to pick me up from my house." She said, pointing the gun at BG.

"Dani put the gun down. Don't let Lenox get in your head. He's a liar."

"Everything you do, every decision you make, benefits you, BG."

"Dani! Put the fuckin gun down!"

"Just say it! Say it, BG!" She yelled.

"Yeah, I did that shit! Yo punk-ass daddy owed me money! I don't give a fuck who it is; they either gon pay up or pay with their life. Yo father chose the latter! Now give me the fuckin gun!" He said, charging at her.

Pow Pow Pow Pow

Dani let four rounds off into BG's chest and stomach. His lifeless body fell to the floor next to Lenox, where Dahlia was holding pressure to his shoulder.

"Dani, call the paramedics, please! Lenox needs help." Dahlia begged her. Dani stood in a daze. She'd offed the love of her life and nearly sent her brother with him. She had been isolated from the world and didn't know where she stood without BG. She closed her eyes and slowly raised the gun to her head.

"Dani, stop!" Dahlia screamed. "Don't let BG win. He lied to you. None of this is your fault—one step at a time. Lenox will survive this, and he'll want to see you when he does. Put the gun down, please." Dahlia pleaded.

EPILOGUE
One Year Later

Lenox raced against the Chicago traffic and time as he weaved in and out of traffic to get to Dahlia. He caught a red-eye from New York to Chicago in hopes of making her graduation on time. With her busy schedule and the new case he was working on, it had been three months since he had seen her other than facetime, of course. He didn't want their first interaction after a lengthy separation to be an argument about him missing her graduation.

Lenox pulled up in front of the United Center, where the ceremony was being held. He got there in just enough time because they were calling her name to walk across the stage after he entered. Lenox cheered along with Naima, who nearly had a front-row seat. After the ceremony, Lenox met Dahlia in the lobby and greeted her with an assortment of dahlias, daisies, and a bouquet of balloons. Dahlia jumped into his arms. She missed the love of her life. She was happy to finally be done with school so she could officially move to New York with him. After all, there was absolutely nothing left in Chicago for her.

"Congratulations, girl." Naima said, handing her a card.

"Thanks, love, and thank you for coming. How're things going?" Naima sighed.

"They're going." She shrugged. "I'm training the new Suga Babies. Tonight's their first event, and you know how that can go."

"Yeah, I do." Dahlia laughed. "Naima, how long are you going to be working for Char. I mean, what happened to Lux and Keena isn't a coincidence. I am not saying Charmaine had something to do with it, but this line of work isn't safe". Though she said what she said to Naima, she was very clear on Charmaine being responsible for their deaths in one way or the other. But Naima had to want to get out of the lifestyle on her own.

"Honestly, I don't know. Charmaine and I recently talked. My contract is up next month, and I am pretty much done training the new girls. So, I could be done with this shit before you know it. Just make sure you save me a spot in your catering company Miss Baller!"

"I got you, boo." Dahlia hugged Naima one last time because she was sure she'd never see her again. Naima would never admit that she was now addicted to the money. Although her contract was up next month, she didn't truly have plans on leaving Charmaine; she saw it in her eyes.

Dahlia and Lenox made sure their late-night flight was squared away before spending the day together. They went to his old studio, where Dahlia had been staying since he had gone back to New York. They made sure everything was packed up for the movers to put into the truck. Dahlia looked at pictures of their new place on her phone and got butterflies in her stomach. She was finally about to say goodbye to Chicago and start her new life with her one and only.

"Okay, so don't be mad."

"What you do now?" Lenox asked Dahlia curiously.

"Nothing. You know I got that event tonight. I'mma just stop by to make sure they're serving the right food and portions before we go."

"Come on, Dahlia, we're going to miss our flight. You know I can't leave Dani unattended for too long. Her psychiatrist said her meds have to be given to her at specific times. If I'm not there, she won't take it."

"Lenox, don't worry. I will meet you at Midway. Our flight leaves at three in the morning. I'll be there at one, trust me. And look, if I'm not, go without me. I'll catch the next one."

"Naw, I'm not leaving you anywhere. If you are not there by one, I'm turning Chicago upside down." He said, kissing her butterfly tattoo, that now covered the spot where BG branded his initials into her.

"Okay, I'll be there. I have to make sure everything goes as planned and tie up loose ends."

Lenox and Dahlia spent the rest of the afternoon intertwined in the sheets. After their multiple trysts, Dahlia got dressed and left the studio. She stood in the shadows, making sure the five workers in the very small catering company were being professional. She tasted all of the food before it went out. The Mardi Gras-themed masquerade ball had a menu full of gumbo, jambalaya, etouffee, Cajun fried chicken, and beignets. She watched as the hotel servers brought out all the food and smiled when the guests complimented the taste. Her job was officially done, but she wanted to talk to the Head Bitch in Charge to make sure *she* was satisfied.

***

Charmaine cut the light on in her office and was startled when she saw Dahlia sitting at her desk.

"I brought you a peace offering." Dahlia said, sliding a beignet over to her mentor.

"No thanks, I'm watching my carb intake." Charmaine replied, setting the beignet to the side.

"Suit yourself," Lia said. "This was a nice event, Char. Are you looking for new talent or just throwing one of your lavish parties as usual?"

"Pretty bold of you to be here, seeing as though you killed my son." Char said, having a seat and staring Dahlia in her eyes.

"I didn't kill him, Charmaine, but if I could relive the moment right before he took his last breath, I would. I wanted to be the one to take him from this world." Charmaine tilted her head at the boldness and audacity of Dahlia. She wasn't surprised at her gall because that's what made her take an interest in the barbie doll in the first place. "Now, Char, I'm just waiting for you to exact revenge." Dahlia continued. "We both know there is no way you'll let your son's killers walk the earth. What do you have planned?" She asked. Charmaine turned around to her liquor decanter and poured herself a drink. She took a sip and continued to entertain the conversation with her former employee.

"Surprisingly, Lia, I prefer to let bygones be bygones. Hasn't there been enough killing and death? Keena, my child, Lux, and even my ex. My business is thriving, and the feds can't touch me even if they tried. Yeah, my one and only son is gone, but that was his own fault. He got greedy. He wanted to keep trophies. And the very person I told him to get rid of was the one who took him out in the end."

"And what about me, Char? You told BG to kill *me*?"

"I'm sure you can understand; I was just protecting my business. You agreed to cooperate with the feds after I had put all my trust in you. Don't play the innocent role with me, Lia."

"No innocent role to play. I was just protecting my life, my dreams. And here I am living them. I cooked the food for the catering company that served you and your guests tonight. I hope we didn't disappoint." Char smiled at Dahlia. She didn't know how to take Dahlia showing up at her office, so she continued to sip her cocktail and listened to her talk. Because at the end of the day, Char was big on tying up loose ends. Lia being in her office alone was the perfect opportunity to do so. The only issue was, she'd just bought the new rug and didn't want Dahlia's blood all over it.

"You know one thing special about being a chef, Char? You can manipulate flavors and textures to get the perfect taste for your dish. It's almost like science."

"I see. And everything was absolutely delicious. Lia, you've done good for yourself. I'm proud of you."

"Thanks, Char, I welcome that compliment. But are you sure that you want your final words in this life to be a compliment to me?"

"Final words?" Charmaine asked, trying to gauge Lia's thought process.

"Yes, final words. Your throat will start to close in about sixty seconds. The beignet was not only covered in the finest powdered sugar—it was infused with the same amount of Pink Ladie pills you stuffed down Lux's throat. Yeah, I figured some things out while I was locked up in your son's villa. But either way, it's kind of poetic, don't you think?"

"Jokes on you, Lia, I didn't eat the beignet, remember? I taught you to be smarter and less predictable than that." she scoffed.

"Yeah, you did teach me that, Charmaine. That's why I put it in your Tequila." She said, winking at her.

Charmaine grabbed her throat in horror. She was losing her breath as her life flashed before her eyes.

When she met Lia in that diner, she didn't know that she was bringing in the woman who would play a part in her demise. Her eyes watered and turned red. Foam lined the corners of her mouth, and dark blood dripped from her nose and lined her ears. She took her final breath and collapsed on her perfect glass desk. Dahlia looked at her mentor, who taught her how to think, move in silence and be the smartest person in the room. She was grateful Char taught her how to play the game of life, though ultimately, it became her undoing in the end.

"Checkmate, Bitch."

The End

About the Author

Daroncia was born and raised in Chicago, Illinois. She graduated with her Master of Social Work from Southern Illinois University of Carbondale. Daroncia spent the early part of her career working with underserved youth in the inner city of Chicago. As a member of Zeta Phi Beta Sorority Inc., Daroncia's goal is to live a life dedicated to service. She continues to serve by advocating for her patients as a Medical Social Worker. Daroncia finds joy in spending time with her family, playing The Sims, writing, and, most of all, reading. Her passion for writing is ignited by those around her.

"I think when you begin to think of yourself as having achieved something, then there's nothing left for you to work towards. I want to believe that there is a mountain so high that I will spend my entire life striving to reach the top of it".

Cicely Tyson

CATALOG

Domino Effect

Marital Bliss

Vegas Heat

Suga Baby

Thank You for reading, stay tuned 😊